SHAKESPEARE NEVER SLEPT HERE

Philip Pleasants as Oberon and Greta Lambert as Titania in the 1985–86 ASF A Midsummer Night's Dream.

SHAKESPEARE NEVER SLEPT HERE

by Jim Volz

The Making of a Regional Theatre

A HISTORY OF THE ALABAMA SHAKESPEARE FESTIVAL

CHEROKEE PUBLISHING COMPANY
Atlanta, Georgia
1986

Library of Congress Cataloging in Publication Data
Volz, Jim, 1953–
    Shakespeare never slept here.

    Includes index.
    1. Alabama Shakespeare Festival—History.
    2. Shakespeare, William, 1564–1616—Stage history—
Alabama.   I. Title.
PN2277.A562A438   1986   792'.09761   85-25482
ISBN 0-87797-118-8 (alk. paper)

This book is printed on acid-free paper which conforms to the American National Stan-dard Z39.48-1984 *Permanence of Paper for Printed Library Materials*. Paper that conforms to this standard's requirements for pH, alkaline reserve and freedom from groundwood is anticipated to last several hundred years without significant deterioration under nor-mal library use and storage conditions. ∞

Manufactured in the United States of America

ISBN: 0-87797-118-8

Classic® binding, R. R. Donnelley & Sons Company. U.S. Patent
No. 4,408,780; Patented in Canada 1984; Patents in other
countries issued or pending.

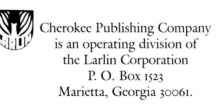 Cherokee Publishing Company
is an operating division of
the Larlin Corporation
P. O. Box 1523
Marietta, Georgia 30061.

Contents

"If this were played upon a stage now, I should condemn it as an improbable fiction."

TWELFTH NIGHT

Foreword

The Alabama Shakespeare Festival has had a unique growth during its first fourteen years. From humble beginnings and a dream in 1971, to the magnificent new complex at Wynfield in Montgomery, the Festival story has been a remarkable one.

It is a story of national proportions and significance, and it is a history of regional interest and pride. An in-depth review of the published literature on theatre reveals a surprising scarcity of information and documentation of America's regional theatres—especially Shakespeare festivals. The available literature on developing and funding new theatre operations is even more limited, and many potential professional theatres have turned to perilous trial-by-error methods in their quest to create reputable operations.

When one considers the typically endless work loads of most theatres' artistic directors and managers, perhaps this scarcity of information is not so surprising. What is remarkable is that this history and exploration of so many facets of the Alabama Shakespeare Festival is surfacing during this dynamic period in the theatre's history. Where did Jim find time to write a book?

There doesn't seem to be a better time than now, as we enter a new era in the ASF saga, to stop and take a long, perhaps sentimental, and sometimes whimsical, look at where we have been.

I vividly remember sitting in the House of Chen, an Anniston landmark restaurant, in the summer of 1982. Jim Volz was in town visiting his wife, ASF actress Evelyn Carol Case, and we all went to dinner. At that time Jim was teaching and directing at the University of Colorado and consulting with a number of professional theatres. As we talked about theatre, art, softball, and management, I remarked, "Jim, ASF really has a great future with the new theatre—you really should come work here," to which Jim replied, with a deft move of his chopsticks, "Call me when the new complex is ready."

Well, I did call Jim a few months later and said, "now." He took the job, and as I write this almost three years later, we are still eagerly awaiting the completion of the theatre. So I lied.

As they say, the rest is history. In the words of one of the ASF's most respected Board members, Austin Letson:

> Jim inherited a floundering Festival and almost singlehandedly turned the situation around. Through his expert leadership and guidance, the Festival was brought into the black and developed into a year-round state theatre. He continually amazed the Board with his ability to solve difficult problems and did so in an entirely professional and exemplary manner.
>
> Jim Volz's administrative abilities rate with the best that I have ever seen in the arts, or other businesses for that matter. The Alabama Shakespeare Festival would certainly not be the dynamic organization that it is today without the expert guidance of Jim Volz.

During the difficult years of transition, Jim has helped guide ASF through the choppy waters of change and growth, from a delightful summer operation in Anniston, to a year-round operation in a $20 million complex in Montgomery. Jim inherited the ASF at its lowest ebb and has helped it to blossom as we head towards an exceptionally bright future. Who better to write our story?

This book is an important event for many, many reasons. To the thousands of people in Anniston who made the Festival possible, this book is an acknowledgment of the blood, sweat, and tears they contributed. To all of the people in Montgomery who are making our transition smooth and exciting, this book is a reminder of where we've been and what the future holds. To the thousands (and I do mean thousands!) of actors, directors, designers, craftspersons, technicians, and administrators who have worked with ASF, it is a testament to their dedication to American regional theatre. To the volunteers who have given hundreds of thousands of hours to ASF, it is an acknowledgment of the power and importance of their work in the past and the future. And to our audiences throughout the Southeast and the nation, it is a history of how one of the nation's smallest theatres became one of the nation's largest.

It truly is time to take stock of where we are and where we have been—and what a great way to do it! Now that the book's done, perhaps it will be easier to get on Jim's appointment calendar—but it was worth it.

Happy reading!

Warmly,

Martin L. Platt,
ASF Artistic Director

Shakespeare Never Slept Here

Top: The home of the ASF's Summer Festival Playhouse in Anniston, Alabama, from 1973 to 1984.

Right: An interior view of the beautiful 1000-seat Festival Playhouse, part of the Anniston Educational Complex.

The Making of a Regional Theatre

The story of the Alabama Shakespeare Festival is a remarkable one as it covers two decades of comedy, laughter, pathos, and tears both on and off stage. It is the tale of a largely volunteer performing arts organization whose humble beginning and opening night performance was delayed "due to technical problems" in a sweltering old high school auditorium. It is an insider's look at a struggling theatre whose actors slept dormitory-style in vacant area hospital rooms and were fed by enthusiastic volunteers who were Shakespeare fans. It is a factual accounting of dramatic delights, depressing deficits, and the triumph of art and willpower over practicality and common sense.

And finally, as is the case with most *happy* histories, it is the story of a professional theatre that survived years of steady, exciting, and sometimes exhausting growth to emerge as one of the nation's largest regional theatres. This is a study of how the ASF has grown, as well as a tribute to those individuals who have made it happen.

The Beginnings in "Annie's Town"

The Alabama Shakespeare Festival opened its first season exactly one hundred years after the birth of Anniston, Alabama. "Annie's Town," as Anniston was first called, was founded in 1872 by two eastern families, and the business of the community consisted mostly of iron ore operations. By 1972, the business and industrial base had diversified, and two military installations, employing thousands of military and civilian personnel, dominated the work force. National industries representing

Charles Antalosky as the Friar in the ASF 1974 undertaking of the tragedy, Romeo and Juliet.

"Here's a marvelous convenient place for our rehearsal."

A MIDSUMMER NIGHT'S DREAM

Martin L. Platt and Board and Guild member, Inga Davis.

An aerial view of ASF's home in the old Anniston High School, demolished in 1982.

chemicals, primary metal, textile products, and fabricated metals supplemented the local industry. The major arts awareness at this time centered on a local community theatre.

It is within this context that a "young whippersnapper" named Martin L. Platt and a small group of followers set the stage for what was to become the State Theatre of Alabama. In 1971, Platt was a twenty-two-year-old theatre enthusiast fresh out of Carnegie Tech in Pittsburgh. A native of Beverly Hills, California, he had worked as the resident director of the Town Meeting Playhouse in Jeffersonville, Vermont, and had free-lanced with individual productions in Los Angeles and Pittsburgh before coming to Anniston to direct the Anniston Community Theatre. Platt soon recognized the opportunity to create a theatre with a professional base that would fill the void of Shakespeare in the southeastern United States. In 1972 and still today, the ASF is the only Shakespeare festival in the Deep South and one of the few professional theatres in the entire Southeast.

In the fall of 1971, the Alabama Shakespeare Festival was only an idea that Platt had been considering, and it wasn't until later that year that he approached the head of the Alabama State Council on the Arts and Humanities. Platt's ideas were enthusiastically received by the Arts Council Executive Director M. J. Zakzrewski, and a grant was requested and received in the early spring of 1972. According to Platt, "Shakespeare festivals had worked in every area of the country but the South, so the chance of success seemed good. Community theatres had a stronghold in the Southeast and normal summer stock theatres didn't have any degree of success because the plays were the same as community theatres . . . Shakespeare was something different."

Platt recalls the first meeting with the Arts Council director as an extremely informal visit:

> The director was in town visiting with a group in Anniston, and we talked about the idea of an Alabama Shakespeare Festival over a bottle of Scotch at a local hotel. At that point they made a commitment to support the project. I'm sure there was a grant application, but the gentlemen's agreement was the important thing.

The Premiere Season

The first tasks involved in the planning of the Alabama Shakespeare Festival were the solicitation and organization of materials from the many other Shakespeare festivals around the country. Platt knew he could learn from studying these materials, researching the opening shows of other festivals, and talking to individuals involved in the producing and directing for other major theatres.

"In selecting the opening season," explains Platt, "I was really trying to find a nice balance while considering what other regional theatres had opened with. For example, the Guthrie Theatre had great success in opening with *Hamlet,* and *Hedda Gabler* seemed to be another good choice in terms of its track record and the enthusiasm many Annistonians had for Ibsen." Major considerations in the first season also included potential cast members, size of the cast, technical limitations, the performance space, and Platt's personal interest and taste. The latter was of the utmost importance, as Platt would eventually direct all four of the first season's shows: *The Two Gentlemen of Verona, The Comedy of Errors, Hamlet,* and *Hedda Gabler.*

In an effort to obtain the best possible actors, Platt borrowed $500 from his mother and used the loan to fly to New York in March 1972. In two days Platt screened applicants chosen from more than two hundred and fifty requests that had been forwarded to him when the ASF plans were announced. According to Platt, his alma mater, Carnegie Tech, was the primary source of actors even though he held extensive non-Equity calls in New York City.

"At the time there were a lot of summer stock theatres that had non-salaried actors," explained Platt. "I have no earthly idea why actors would work for no money, but what we had to offer was classical theatre work, the housing and hospitality of the citizens of Anniston, and the opportunity to work in repertory." While recruiting actors, Platt shared his dream of establishing the only Shakespeare festival between Dallas

"To show our simple skill, This is the true beginning of our end."

A MIDSUMMER NIGHT'S DREAM

and Washington, D.C., and pushed his view that it was possible to make Shakespeare work in a Deep South town of less than 30,000 people. "I persuaded some fine actors who were friends, as well as some other support staff, to commit themselves to the idea and spend the summer in Anniston," he recalled. Platt also insists that, despite his mother's pleas, he did indeed pay her back for that original loan!

The services of three young designers were enlisted from Birmingham, Atlanta, and Minneapolis. "I didn't want to hire other directors," explains Platt. "No one else would hire me to direct these plays so I decided to do them myself."

The casting and repertory rehearsal process was an exhausting and rigorous process. "Back in those days before we were hiring members of the Actor's Equity Association, there weren't any union regulations. You could rehearse twelve to thirteen hours a day," recalls Platt. "Each show had its own slot. There weren't any days off. We had approximately 120 hours per show to rehearse, but nobody complained because we were all committed to the task at hand."

Although Platt describes the first year's efforts as "small shows with a

ASF Madrigal Singers in Anniston at a "Music at St. Michael's" concert.

4

Members of Anniston's ASF Guild attending an annual wine and cheese party.

Three of Anniston's Junior Guild members preparing for lobby duties prior to an ASF performance.

Enthusiastic Anniston Junior Guild members.

Judith Marx (right) and friend.

scruffy company," he is quick to emphasize the year's successes and his respect for the company and community. Prior to the opening of the first season, he articulated what would be the first and most rudimentary of many manifestos concerning the Alabama Shakespeare Festival:

> The Alabama Shakespeare Festival is truly a great challenge. We are here in a part of the country where Shakespeare in production is almost nonexistent. Almost everyone remembers Shakespeare unpleasantly from high school and college English classes, and what we must do is present Shakespeare in a way which will make these people forget their prejudices. Shakespeare is first and foremost an entertaining playwright, not an oblique poet. He was writing for a mass audience, not a select one. I think that once people learn how much fun Shakespeare can be, by coming to one performance, they will be fans for the whole season.

In his program notes for 1972, Platt writes that *The Comedy of Errors* "may not, as critics suggest, be one of Shakespeare's finest or maturest works, but for sheer zaniness and entertainment, it is certainly a delight for this or any age. The wild, uninhibited comic performances of the ancient Romans gave birth to much of what we still laugh at today."

In an effort to highlight the "wit and elegance" of *The Two Gentlemen of Verona,* Platt set the production in the 1830s, the era just preceding Victoria's rise to the throne of England. The production of *Hamlet* took on the look of "medieval Denmark through modern eyes." According to Platt, a black-and-white motif was chosen for *Hamlet* to help sharpen the lines between Hamlet's two major periods in the play.

The Alabama Shakespeare Festival's Hamlet was "a sensitive, intelligent young prince seeking proof through action" as opposed to "the story of a man beset with inaction and melancholy." *Hedda Gabler* took advantage of the early 1970s social issues; Platt felt that "with women's rights again in the news, it is important to present this play, which deals so seriously and effectively with the problems faced by a woman in a male-dominated society."

Opening Night

As it turns out, Hamlet wasn't the only Anniston character beset with inaction and melancholy. It seems that Alabama was inactive and Platt was melancholic. The reason? On opening night only two people sat in the audience—a critic and his wife!

The opening performance in the unair-conditioned theatre was unmercifully delayed while the company finished sewing the costumes for the show (*Hamlet*)! The trend seemed destined to continue as the dog who played Crab in the following show, *The Two Gentlemen of Verona*, ran away twice! The first time, "Mr. Nook," a southern Shakespeare dog, ended up in the dog pound and on the front page of the city newspaper. The second time, Artistic Director Platt put his foot down and had him replaced by his understudy.

However, there was no stopping Martin Platt and the ASF staff! Brandishing an acting company of eleven men and four women, Platt barreled into the rest of the season, which was first hesitantly then enthusiastically received by supporters and audiences. Although the local paper hailed *The Comedy of Errors* as "high spirited and inventive" and *Hamlet* as "eminently worth waiting for," another local critic would later write that "the first season of the Festival in 1972 was so bad I didn't bother coming back for the second." According to this last critic, "the theatre was hot, the production values nil, and the straight-out-of-college cast ran the gamut from hopeless to promising." Indeed it was true that the first season was performed in a dilapidated, unair-conditioned, abandoned high school, where temperatures easily soared into the 100s, sapping the energies of audiences and performers. The old Anniston High School auditorium doubled as a basketball court, and the stage was obviously more accustomed to basketball players than actors. In fact, reporter Thomas Noland wrote that "by the end of the season, many of the 3,000 who saw those plays wondered if the Alabama Shakespeare Festival would be remembered as an honorable failure of the summer of '72." However, according to the national publication, *The Shakespeare Complex,* "In spite of all the negative factors, by the end of their first season, audience response indicated that the Anniston area was ready for Shakespeare."

"Who can control his fate?"

OTHELLO

Left: Charles Antalosky, Sebastian Russ, and William Miller in Shakespeare's Richard II, *1975.*

Below: Members of the 1975 cast of Twelfth Night.

8

Lester Malizia (left) and Ronald Sopyla (right) in the Alabama Shakespeare Festival's production of Feydeau's Fitting for Ladies, *1975.*

Kathleen Forbes in the ASF's 1976 comedy,
The Merry Wives of Windsor.

Governing Forces

A distinguished Board of Governors headed by Mrs. George (Cornelia) Wallace helped the Festival break into its first season. Representatives from local universities, the Anniston newspaper, The Birmingham theatres, the business community, and the Alabama State Arts Council were appointed to the Board of Governors and helped spread the word about Alabama's first venture into professional classical theatre and Shakespeare festivals. Alabama Shakespeare Festival Board member Josephine E. Ayers describes the earliest days of the Festival:

> The condition of the Festival's birth and life describes the responsibility of the Board of Directors. Unlike other important regional theatres, the Alabama Shakespeare Festival did not spring from the spacious treasury of the Ford Foundation or from any other major funding source. In the cultural life of Alabama and the South it was a frontier institution with a frontier budget.

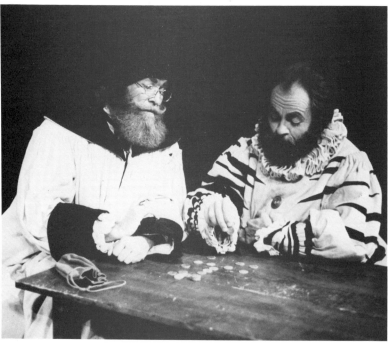

Richard Grupenhoff and Charles Antalosky in the ASF's 1976 production of The Merry Wives of Windsor.

Andrew Cole and Mark Varian in the 1976 ASF production of The Winter's Tale.

The early years of the Alabama Shakespeare Festival are eloquently recalled by Thomas Noland:

> When Martin L. Platt, Founder and Artistic Director of the Alabama Shakespeare Festival, brought William Shakespeare to Anniston seven summers ago, few shook the playwright's hand and fewer still embraced him. He was, after all, an imposing visitor. He peered out of woodcuts and paintings like a somber judge, and he talked, as one theatregoer told me, "like a book." Most people doubted he would be any different from the haughty, stiff fellow they remembered in the high school editions of his works, and although Platt did his best to change that notion, only 3,000 called on him that summer in his cramped and stuffy quarters at the old Anniston High School.

The imposing visitor that Noland recalls ended up in the hands of Martin L. Platt and fell prey to a series of bold and risky productions that would later be labeled as "a factor in our thriving, growing success." The boldness could take the form of changes in locale, anachronistic music and songs, or exotic interpretations. However, Platt is quick to note that, although the Alabama Shakespeare Festival wanted to make the plays "live for modern audiences," the text is always "Shakespeare word for word."

It should be emphasized that a major factor in the Alabama Shakespeare Festival's early success and mounting enthusiasm was simple geography. Although Anniston seemed an unlikely spot for Shakespeare, it was the only major Shakespeare festival in the southeastern United States, conveniently located on the main highway between Birmingham and Atlanta. Chattanooga, Tennessee, is also within easy striking distance, and Anniston is a quick detour for anyone traveling from the Midwest or Northeast to the Gulf Coast.

The first season of the Alabama Shakespeare Festival ran for thirty-one performances and, despite a forty-five minute delay in the opening night production of *Hamlet* to finish costumes, the season played without any major problems. At the end of the season a spokesman for the Festival wrote that "the mammoth undertaking of organizing the Festival and directing all four of the productions without a full-time staff was not only accomplished, but the 1972 Festival was a resounding success."

The Second Season

Once the Alabama Shakespeare Festival proved that ongoing summer Shakespeare had potential in the South, community groups, local businessmen, and many Calhoun County arts supporters decided to capitalize on the excitement generated by the first season and work to form a

Top: Richard Grupenhoff and Charles Anta-losky in the ASF's nationally acclaimed 1976 production of the tragedy, King Lear.

Below: Stefan Cotner and Robert Rieben in King Lear, *1976.*

Right: The Earl of Gloucester is tortured by the evil Regan, portrayed by Richard Grupen-hoff and Elizabeth Schuette in the Alabama Shakespeare Festival's 1976 production of King Lear.

12

Board of Directors, formally incorporate, and expand to a beautiful new theatre recently constructed as part of the Anniston Educational Park Complex. An ambitious season of *Much Ado About Nothing, Macbeth, As You Like It,* and *Tartuffe* was slated from July 12 through August 11, 1973. Platt remained in charge of the Festival and again decided to direct all four productions.

A note tucked away in one of Platt's old programs details his thoughts going into the second season:

> Directing four plays of the magnitude of our 1973 presentations is a major responsibility. I must serve each production with equal enthusiasm and care. What helps in doing this is that when the season is selected, the plays which are chosen are ones that will appeal not only to our audiences, but also ones that will excite my imagination so that I may focus all of my resources on the productions. What some people may fail to realize is that before our four-week rehearsal period, my staff of designers and technicians and I spend almost three months in preparation for the season, so that when rehearsals roll around, everything is ready for the actors. All the legwork is completed.

Despite the young cast, the Alabama Shakespeare Festival was determined to be accepted as a professional theatre. The pursuit of high artistic standards, production consistency, and strong, flexible actors was the obvious key to success.

In 1973, the acting company expanded from fifteen to twenty-five and included a number of actors with strong performance credentials and experience in classical theatre and Shakespeare. The season itself was highly influenced by the trends of the time in regional and New York theatre, with the Alabama Shakespeare Festival's rock version of *As You Like It* corresponding with Joseph Papp's musical *Two Gentlemen of Verona*, and a *Gone With the Wind* version of *Much Ado About Nothing* being influenced by a New York Shakespeare Festival production of *Much Ado About Nothing* a la Teddy Roosevelt.

The 1973 *Much Ado About Nothing* featured a "Tara-esque" setting and was costumed in Civil War hoop skirts, gray military uniforms, and "dashing cutaway coats" from the 1860s. Music from the period was also interwoven into the production to "make this a truly memorable, southern production of one of Shakespeare's truly great comedies."

Platt's 1973 *As You Like It* took even greater liberties. It was billed by the Festival as the "world premiere of a rock musical version of Shakespeare's great comedy." According to Platt, "The play, a delightful mixture of fantasy and romance, lends itself beautifully to music. The production was costumed in colorful, contemporary designs with "bows to the Elizabethan era," and sported long hair, sandals, and beach balls.

Behind the scenes, Platt and the actors were certain that the show was a disaster. As one company member explains it, "We faced opening night as if we were facing a firing squad!"

As You Like It, in this rock romp form, caught the fancy of critics and audience members alike. *The Anniston Star* review posted the week after the opening states that "the main problem with William Shakespeare's brilliant comedy *As You Like It* is simply that it had to wait nearly four hundred years to be presented as winningly as it was last Saturday night at the new Anniston High School auditorium." The reporter describes the Alabama Shakespeare Festival production as "miraculous," "remarkably detailed," and deserving of "nothing less than standing room only audiences."

One out-of-state reporter noted that "music reverberated via a combo much smaller than its sound, positioned touching-close to (sic) the theatre entrance, setting the rock opera mood. . . . as with all ASF productions, not a line or intonation varied from the original. . . . Shakespeare, the great playwright, the great wit, the great educator proved not an immortal to revere, but a universal master of delight, a quality Anniston's theatre directors exploited for abundant audience benefit."

More traditional productions of *Macbeth* and *Tartuffe* rounded out the Festival's second season, which, according to Festival Board President B. C. Moore, reflected "part of a rebirth of interest in Shakespeare's plays which is taking place all over the English-speaking world."

A Guild Is Formed

From the beginning, members of the Anniston community reached out and nurtured the ASF company, bringing them into their homes for the summer, feeding them between performances, introducing them to the diverse joys of Alabama, and treating them to the best in southern hospitality. The ASF Guild, first organized by Betty Potts on August 1, 1973, helped promote, support, and stimulate interest in the ASF and proved vital to the success of the Festival throughout the year. Consistently numbering nearly two hundred women, the Guild sponsored after-theatre parties, hostessed every performance, and helped sew costumes, gather properties, and contribute in many ways to the artistic success of the theatre.

The Alabama Shakespeare Festival Guild furnished volunteer help as requested by the Festival Board and the professional staff. Each year, Guild members spent more than 7,000 hours in a myriad of activities, such as working in the Festival office, serving matinee suppers for the

Above: ASF's 1978 production of Measure for Measure *with William Verdeber, Mark Varian, and James Donadio.*

Left: Mark Varian and Dennis Bateman in The Comedy of Errors, *1979.*

Festival company, and providing refreshments for the Thursday night Meet-the-Actors parties. The Guild also hosted an annual party to welcome the company members. Members, aided by their husbands, served as hostesses at each performance, welcoming theatre patrons and selling programs and souvenirs. A Guild committee lavishly decorated the lobby, setting up plants, banners, and displays. The Guild's Trunk Committee gathered household necessities to help make the company members' brief stay more comfortable and enjoyable. The Guild's Lodging Committee coordinated company members' accommodations in Anniston homes as well as visitors' requests for lodging. Other committees sought out unusual stage properties and sold program ads. These enthusiastic volunteers made an invaluable contribution to the growth and success of the Festival throughout the 1970s and 1980s. Their continual support was truly essential.

Why Shakespeare at All?

Many of the articles and public relations materials generated by the Alabama Shakespeare Festival staff and volunteers in the early years were designed to help educate area audiences and enlighten community leaders to the joys of Shakespeare. As one 1973 program note queried, "Why a Shakespeare Festival at all? Isn't it boring enough to have to study Shakespeare in school, without having to be subjected to him in the summer?" Audience education was an important factor in audience

Charles Antalosky as Shylock in the 1978 production of The Merchant of Venice.

Sydney Hibbert in the title role of Othello, *1978.*

Left: Sydney Hibbert in the 1978 production of The Merchant of Venice.

Below, left: Richard Levine and Michele Farr in the title roles of ASF's Romeo and Juliet, *1980.*

Below, right: Bruce Cromer and Ellen Fiske in the 1980 production of The Two Gentlemen of Verona.

Jacob Harran as Puck and Steven Sutherland as Oberon in the 1981 ASF production of A Midsummer Night's Dream.

Richard Levine as Romeo and Michele Farr as Juliet at ASF in 1980.

The Making of a Regional Theatre   17

building and appreciation of Shakespeare's plays, and Artistic Director Platt addressed the task as part of his 1973 statement of purpose:

> These characters were written to be acted on the stage, and to be acted so as to relate to the audiences which saw them—Elizabethan audiences. So, today, the Alabama Shakespeare Festival is trying to revive the original spirit of Shakespeare, the spirit of entertainment, of amusement. Our goal is to make the plays live for 1973 audiences. . . . the transformation from archaic literature to dramas of clarity and wit is accomplished through the skill of the actors, the director, and the technicians and designers.

The Mid-1970s

Platt continued his solo hold on production direction until 1974 when Bruce Hoard directed an "apprentice production" of Machiavelli's *Mandragola.* The production pleased Platt, and he invited Hoard back again in 1975 as an "associate director" to perform in three productions, teach acting classes, and direct the apprentice production of *Ralph Roister Doister.* Finally, in 1976, Hoard became only the second individual to direct for the Alabama Shakespeare Festival main-stage season as Platt hired him to take the helm of *The Merry Wives of Windsor.*

The years between 1973 and 1976 heralded a consistent upgrading of the quality of the artistic company. The number of actors involved in the company ranged from twenty to thirty-seven. The Alabama Shakespeare Festival company produced *A Midsummer Night's Dream, Romeo and Juliet, The Taming of the Shrew,* and Molière's *The School for Wives* in 1974; and *The Tempest, Richard II, Twelfth Night,* and Feydeau's *Fitting for Ladies* in 1975.

In a note to audience members, Platt credits a larger budget as resulting in an "increasingly polished and professional level of performance" and notes that "theatre fans from every state in the Southeast" are attending the Festival.

In 1974 Platt's artistic objectives began to take a clearer form:

> An underlying idea of the Festival is to familiarize the public with Shakespeare and widen the appeal of a man who is, at his best, a very down-to-earth playwright. For Shakespeare belongs not only to the academics: the true greatness of his plays can best be appreciated by seeing and hearing his plays acted—not only by reading and studying them. In these first three seasons, I have attempted to present a cross-section of the Bard's plays and find a specific production scheme for each play that will enhance the important qualities of each play for contemporary audiences.

Platt's production scheme seemed to be paying off as the Alabama Shakespeare Festival began attracting attention from throughout the

Robert Browning and Shannon Eubanks in the ASF's 1980 comedy, The Importance of Being Earnest.

Southeast. Thomas Noland writes that it was the 1974 "lavish, brilliant *A Midsummer Night's Dream* which changed the tone of newspaper reviews from condescending approval to genuine admiration." According to Noland, "Platt in a sense had taught himself to direct and his company responded superbly. *Romeo and Juliet, The Taming of the Shrew,* Molière's *The School for Wives,* and Machiavelli's *Mandragola* combined with *A Midsummer Night's Dream* for a season lauded by *The National Observer* in Washington, as well as by *The Birmingham News* and other Alabama journals."

In a news story entitled, "WHAT LIGHT THROUGH YONDER WINDOW BREAKS, Y'ALL?", *The National Observer* raved about the Alabama Shakespeare Festival's "funny, imaginatively staged" *A Midsummer Night's Dream,* "action filled" *Romeo and Juliet,* and "tempestuous" *The Taming of the Shrew.* "The 26-year-old director and his company are doing an especially commendable job winning the hearts and minds for Shakespeare hereabouts," wrote *The National Observer*'s Bruce Cook. "And they are doing it by bringing him to ever-growing audiences in good, thoroughly professional productions."

Kenneth Shorey of *The Birmingham News* also summarized the strength of the 1974 season in a glowing report:

> Wasn't it Sir Tyrone Guthrie who said it's time to take Shakespeare out of our schools and put him back on the stage where he belongs? This season's Anniston Festival is doing just that: giving us an athletic, bawdy, robust, noisy Shakespeare "for the whole family," as the phrase is, on a brand new open platform stage a la the Canadian Stratford, in rich dazzling Alan Armstrong costumes like you wouldn't believe! There was a standing ovation opening night for *A Midsummer Night's Dream,* as much for Alan Armstrong and the splendor of Martin Platt's vision as for the actors collectively. . . . the overall effect of what we see virtually rivals the three

James Donadio in Wilde's comedy, The Importance of Being Earnest, *1981.*

Welcoming party for the 1980 company, hosted by the Alabama Shakespeare Festival Guild.

Robert C. Torri (left) and Cathy Brewer-Moore (above) in the 1981 ASF musical Oh, Coward!

Evelyn Carol Case as Ophelia in ASF's Marowitz version of Hamlet, *1981.*

Donna Haley as Beatrice Rasponi and Steven Sutherland as Pantalone in the comedy The Servant of Two Masters.

Byron Hays, A. D. Cover, Charles Antalosky, and William Preston in the 1981 ASF comedy, A Midsummer Night's Dream.

Stratfords (Ontario, Connecticut, and on-Avon) and serves to establish Anniston as the next likely site for a permanent Festival in North America.

Even Alabama Governor George C. Wallace sent a congratulatory note to the Alabama Shakespeare Festival for "the outstanding work that you have done to enable many of our citizens to enjoy this wonderful classic entertainment."

The 1974 offerings were in a more traditional vein than in previous years. Platt began to emphasize his belief in keeping Shakespeare intact and in not unnecessarily editing or changing time settings. "This year (1974)," writes Platt, "we have done almost no cutting at all and we have fun with the plays in their period. Sometimes people twist them so far out of their periods that they no longer mean the same things." These notes signaled a change in his production approach to the classics that would be echoed throughout the 1970s and 1980s.

Stating artistic objectives involves clarity of thought, purpose, and a pencil or typewriter. Achieving artistic objectives oftentimes involves magic, miracles, and manpower. Various problems and barriers to

Anne Sandoe, Shannon Eubanks, and Jane Moore in Molière's Tartuffe, *1980.*

achieving stated production goals inevitably surface and demand solutions. Following a series of conversations with Platt, the editors of *The Shakespeare Complex* wrote, "In the first three summers of its existence, the ASF underwent considerable change and growth. The shoestring operation of the first year became a modestly produced Festival the second year—one with difficulties to overcome but considerable potential. The designers and the director were quite visibly not comfortable with the stage they had to work with."

To combat this problem, a new thrust stage was designed in 1975 for the extension of the basic proscenium high school stage and for the elevation of the actors, which would allow for a more intimate relationship between actor and audience. At the same time, public relations officials for the 1975 season noted that "this year, the productions will have more elaborate settings and costumes and the audiences will be privileged to enjoy a quality of performances equal to other Shakespeare festivals in the country." Alabama Shakespeare Festival Board President William J. Davis greeted Festival visitors with a letter expressing his belief that "Shakespeare festivals are becoming more and more popular, and we are proud that we are able to offer a festival that compares most favorably with the other three major Festivals in the country. The Alabama Shakespeare Festival is the only one of its type in the entire Southeast and we are pleased that all neighboring states are represented in our list of season ticket holders."

Each passing year seemed to clarify the artistic intention and goals of the founder of the Alabama Shakespeare Festival. In a 1975 publication directed to audience members, Platt wrote:

> The purpose of the Festival is to bring the plays of Shakespeare to the people of Alabama and the Greater Southeast in entertaining and professional productions. It is an ambitious project, and one without precedent in this region. As the only professional theatre in the state, we have developed a reputation out of our company style: presenting witty, elegant, earthy, and sometimes bawdy productions of Shakespeare's plays that entertain a vast cross-section of people in the Southeast. The Alabama Shakespeare Festival is not only for those who are familiar with the Bard, but also for that vast majority that were "turned off" to Shakespeare because they were forced to read the plays that were only written to be heard. Shakespeare was a popular playwright in his day, enjoyed for the most part by the common man, paying a minimal price to see the plays. And it is still to the basic human instincts that Shakespeare appeals, prompting laughter, tears, and all the emotions from people of all walks of life. What we have tried to accomplish at the Festival is to evoke these feelings in every member of our audiences, entertaining and exciting them through our productions.

"I had rather hear my dog bark at a crow than a man swear he loves me."

MUCH ADO ABOUT NOTHING

Preceding page, top: Charles Antalosky (left), Judy Langford, and Richard Ruskell (right) in the 1981 production of The Servant of Two Masters.

Preceding page, bottom: Karen Bauder and Catherine Moore (left) and William Preston (right) in Much Ado About Nothing, *1981.*

Left: Carol Haynes and Sheree Galpert in Two Gentlemen of Verona, *1980.*

Below: Donna Haley and Arthur Hanket in the ASF's 1981 production of the history, Henry IV, Part One.

Left: Robert Browning, Cathy Brewer-Moore (pictured again on right), and Robert C. Torri in the 1981 ASF musical accomplishment, Oh, Coward!

National Recognition in 1976

In process and in retrospect, 1976 marked a milestone and major breakthrough for the Alabama Shakespeare Festival as the State Theatre created its first working relationship with the Actor's Equity Association, hired its first guest director, produced its first "thoroughly successful tragedy" and received its first *New York Times* review. The review labeled Platt "a brash, brilliant director" and reported that *King Lear* "tore and wrenched the audience" who "rose to their feet shouting" during the final bows. *Shakespeare Quarterly*'s Carol McGinnis Kay hailed Charles Anatolsky's King Lear as "the standard by which I'll judge all future performances" and lauded the ASF production for "showing us the beast unleashed and in so doing achieved one of those rare evenings of power for which we all keep returning to the live theatre."

Charles Antalosky was the first Equity actor contracted by the Alabama Shakespeare Festival and the only equity actor in 1976. The season itself was a challenging spectacle with a nineteenth-century European version of *The Winter's Tale* and fairly straightforward presentations of *The Merry Wives of Windsor, King Lear,* and Molière's *The Miser.*

1976 will also go down in ASF history as the year of the great power failures. On one fateful Saturday, with a sold-out matinee house, 1,000 audience members were stranded for nearly two hours in a blackened auditorium. The actors set up impromptu dressing tables in the sunlit lobby area, and the waiting audience loved it!

A number of important additions to the theatre offerings helped add to the Alabama Shakespeare Festival's reputation as a "festival" in the truest sense during the mid-to-late 1970s. The ASF's expansion included a commitment to a touring program, a chamber music series, a film series, and other special events that helped create a festive atmosphere in Anniston, Alabama, and in surrounding states for much longer than the original four to six weeks. In 1976, the ASF sponsored "The Great American Shakespeare Sale" as a bicentennial project and first venture into touring in-state and out-of-state. Due to limited funds, the ASF decided that instead of touring a play, they would introduce large numbers of people to the Festival through a strolling troupe of players in Elizabethan dress.

The Governor's Proclamation

Sandwiched between The Great American Shakespeare Sale and the next summer season was a monumental moment in the history of the Alabama Shakespeare Festival. On June 17, 1977, Governor George C. Wallace proclaimed the ASF "the State Theatre of Alabama" in recognition of the theatre's quality and reputation. This proclamation helped lend credibility and support, artistically and financially, to the ASF and set the stage for a number of crucial developments. Positive mention of the pivotal 1976 season in both *The New York Times* and *The Washington Post,* strong public relations created by the Great American Shakespeare Sale, and the Governor's acclamation all helped rally community spokesmen, civic leaders, and the Board of Directors behind the ASF even more strongly than before.

William Preston and James Donadio in the 1981 ASF production of the comedy, A Midsummer Night's Dream.

From ASF's 1981 A Midsummer Night's Dream, *Charles Antalosky as Bottom (opposite)* and Jacob Harran and Steven Sutherland as Puck and Oberon *(above).*

Left: Karen Bauder and Deborah Fezelle in the hit comedy, A Midsummer Night's Dream, *1981.*

Below: Arthur Hanket and Deborah Fezelle as Shakespeare's young lovers in A Midsummer Night's Dream, *1981.*

For the first time, plays by living playwrights surfaced in the season's offerings. Tom Stoppard's *Rosencrantz and Guildenstern Are Dead,* and David Rintel's *Clarence Darrow* turned up in 1977 and 1978. An entertainment on the "foibles and fall of the Kings and Queens of England" devised by John Barton of the Royal Shakespeare Company rounded out the 1977 season. Two musical adaptations of period poetry entitled *A Lover's Complaint* and *Oh, William!* added a light touch to the 1978 and 1979 seasons, which included such heavyweights as *Othello, Measure for Measure,* and *The Merchant of Venice.*

Help from Professional Friends

As the ASF's repertory expanded and developed, it became increasingly important for the theatre to work toward full professional status as a League of Resident Theatres (LORT) member. One of the crucial events that signaled the beginning of this journey was an offer from the Foundation for the Extension and Development of the American Professional Theatre (FEDAPT) to help develop the structure of the ASF as the Festival's first step toward LORT membership. FEDAPT supplied a wide range of consultants, including management personnel from the Guthrie Theatre and the McCarter Theatre and also helped frame the contractual agreements that assisted the Festival in the development of its Equity/LORT status. These consultancies lasted for approximately three years, and it was during this time that the Alabama

Left: Shakespeare's rustics cavort onstage in the ASF production of the comedy, A Midsummer Night's Dream, *1981.*

Below: John-Frederick Jones in A Midsummer Night's Dream, *1981.*

Shakespeare Festival attained the schedule and status of a full-fledged professional theatre.

Frederic B. Vogel, Executive Director of FEDAPT, requested in his first meeting with the ASF Board of Directors that all parties "do a little bit more investigation and identification of what the Alabama Shakespeare Festival is and importantly, why do you want it, and what do you want to accomplish?" These questions were important ones for the Alabama Shakespeare Festival, and the next five years would be spent grappling with how to become what the Artistic Director wanted it to be—a successful, classical repertory theatre operating on a year-round basis with a resident company.

Professional Training for Young Actors

Platt's emphasis in the middle-to-late seventies was on developing a company of actors to work in rotating repertory. He wished to continue the ensemble concept that had been so important to the beginnings of the regional theatre movement. The reliance on thoroughly professional

Left: Charles Antalosky in the title role of the ASF's first Chekhov production, Uncle Vanya, *in 1982.*

Below, left: The ASF's 1980 version of Cymbeline.

Below, right: Shannon Eubanks as Hippolyta in A Midsummer Night's Dream, *1981.*

Opposite: Evelyn Carol Case and Bruce Cromer on tour with ASF throughout the Southeastern states, in the title roles in Romeo and Juliet, *1982.*

The Making of a Regional Theatre   33

Equity actors helped solidify the base of the ASF company at the same time that younger actors were being groomed for larger assignments in the years to come. The Alabama Shakespeare Festival Acting Conservatory Training Program established in 1978 was the most important single element in the development of younger actors within the Festival structure. The program was set up for twenty students, aged twenty to thirty, who were professionally oriented and intending to pursue a career in regional theatre. Classes in acting, movement, voice, Shakespeare, fencing, and directing were integrated with experience in small roles during the season as a way of training "students to become full-time members of the professional company."

According to ASF officials, the Conservatory was born out of the conviction that the Festival needed to serve the southeastern region by making its educational and cultural resources available to the greater community. It was also created in an effort to develop a pool of professional actors and directors in the Southeast. In the first year, the conservatory consisted of ten students taking classes from seven faculty members and two guest lecturers. The printed goals for the program included giving "each student a discipline to carry with him which will continue to help him in his professional development and to give him basic training and experience."

Left: Charles Antalosky in the 1982 production of A Servant of Two Masters.

Opposite: Charles Antalosky as Friar Lawrence comforting Evelyn Carol Case as Juliet in Romeo and Juliet, *1982.*

Evelyn Carol Case on tour as Juliet during the 1982 ASF southeast tour of Romeo and Juliet.

Costume plates designed by Lynne Emmert for the 1979 ASF production of As You Like It.

Above: John-Frederick Jones, Jacob Harran, and Bruce Cromer in ASF's 1981 production of Henry IV, Part One.

Left: James Donadio and William Preston in ASF's A Midsummer Night's Dream, *1981.*

Michele Farr embraces Bruce Cromer in the 1982 ASF production of the tragedy, Hamlet.

Below: John O'Neal as Junebug Jabbo Jones, *1982.*

Right: Linda Stephens and John-Frederick Jones in Hamlet, *1982.*

A number of Alabama universities also capitalized on the artistic and educational benefits and resources of the ASF by scheduling class visits, tours, and workshops throughout the summer. Jacksonville State University, one of the largest Alabama universities, even scheduled a "Shakespeare Onstage" three-credit graduate English course in cooperation with the ASF. This course featured lectures by distinguished Shakespearean scholars, conferences with ASF actors and the Artistic Director, study of representative Shakespearean plays, and attendance at performances of all the Shakespeare-related plays.

ASF and the All-America City

By 1978, the Board of Directors had grown to over twenty, and additional volunteers numbered in the hundreds. The support that the citizens of Anniston and the surrounding communities of Oxford and Jacksonville gave to Platt and the Festival was paying off in many ways, but perhaps the jackpot was the City of Anniston's notification on March 30, 1978, that the National Municipal League had awarded the City the prestigious All-America City award. Anniston was cited for its development of a broad leadership coalition action group to defuse community problems and for its "miracle of the Alabama Shakespeare Festival."

The community pride and long-term economic effects generated by this major national award endeared the Festival to the community to an

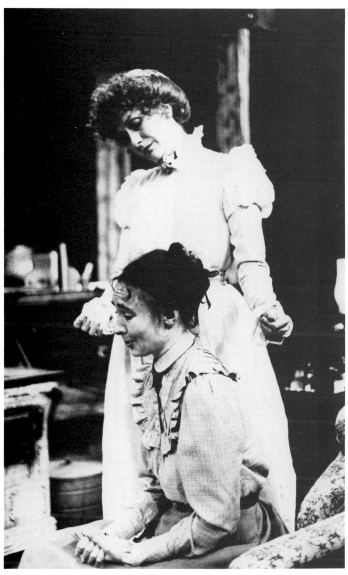

Frank Raiter (above) and John-Frederick Jones (below) perform Chekhov's Uncle Vanya, *1982.*

Michele Farr (seated) and Linda Stephens in Chekhov's Uncle Vanya, *1982.*

even greater extent, and the push for bigger and better productions continued. In 1978, Josephine E. Ayers joined the ASF staff as Executive Producer, and the ASF budget grew to over $250,000 as the company sported eleven Equity contracts, an increase of ten in two years. The artistic design staff also contributed in major ways to the development of the Festival in the late 1970s as set and lighting designer Michael Stauffer and costume designer Lynne Emmert created what Platt would later call "the ASF look." According to Platt, "Lynne and Michael are two of the people who helped put us on the map. They are both designers who are able to get the most product out of the least money and are good staff motivators."

On the Road

The artistic team of Michael Stauffer, Lynne Emmert, and Martin L. Platt mounted the ASF's first major tour of a Shakespeare production in the fall of 1978. *The Taming of the Shrew,* last produced by the Alabama Shakespeare Festival in 1974, was selected as the touring vehicle. The six-week journey extended across seven southeastern states and helped establish the ASF as the key theatre group in the region. Touring high schools, colleges, and communities in Alabama, Mississippi, Louisiana, Florida, Georgia, Tennessee, and Kentucky, *The Taming of the Shrew* played to audiences, "many of whom have never before seen Shakespeare performed." Kenneth Shorey of *The Birmingham News* lauded its "overall brilliance of design and conception," and the Columbus, Georgia, *Enquirer* called it "sensational, assisted by the most exquisite array of costumes and effective off-stage musical accompaniment."

The Taming of the Shrew would soon be followed by Shakespeare and non-Shakespeare touring productions that would help promote the artistic achievements of the ASF regionally and nationally. *Twelfth Night* visited ten states in eleven weeks in 1979; *The Two Gentlemen of Verona* toured for twelve weeks in 1980; *The Importance of Being Earnest* toured for ten weeks in 1981; *Romeo and Juliet* toured for eight weeks in 1982; *The Comedy of Errors* toured for seven weeks in 1983; *Arms and the Man* toured for seven weeks in 1984; and *The Glass Menagerie* tours in 1986. The touring productions have reached nearly a quarter of a million people over the years, and it is well documented that the ASF has traveled into many communities that had never been exposed to professional theatre. Managing Director Anne Zimmerman summarized the overall value of touring in a description of the 1978 production:

> The production—*The Taming of the Shrew*—played to a variety of audiences: junior high and high school students, college students, prison inmates, small communities, large communities. Some were prepared for what they saw; others were not. But they all enjoyed the performance and left with new knowledge of and appreciation for Shakespeare and for theatre. . . . The Festival has a commitment to serve the state and region, to make its cultural and educational resources easily accessible, and to educate future audiences. Touring with high quality theatre—theatre of the same quality as that which the Festival produces during the resident season in Anniston—is one way in which the Festival strives to meet that responsibility.

John-Frederick Jones and Michele Farr in Uncle Vanya, *1982.*

John-Frederick Jones and Linda Stephens in Uncle Vanya, *1982.*

The Late 1970s

In 1979, Platt looked back on the first seven years of the Festival and presented a new challenge:

> The growth of the Festival has been very rapid in every area, and as we enter our eighth season, the results of this growth will be more obvious than ever before. Perhaps most important has been our continued artistic growth. We are most fortunate at the Festival to have been able to grow and mature artistically under very favorable conditions and to have created an atmosphere in which it is a joy to be engaged in the creative process. It has from the beginning been the policy of the Festival to strive for the best possible performances of the plays we produce. It has taken many years for us to reach the point at which it is economically feasible to provide all of the right components to achieve this goal. But as we move toward the end of the Festival's first decade, the goal is clearly in sight. The Festival is now in the position, as the leading classic repertory theatre in this region, to attract the finest actors, designers, directors, and craftsmen working in the theatre in America today. As we have grown, both what I expect as Artistic Director and what you expect as our audience has changed. We are all a bit more sophisticated now, a bit more discerning, and as we have grown with the Festival, we have demanded more and more from the productions.

The continual challenge, then, is for continued and improved standards of excellence. As we expand our season and our repertoire, we challenge our audience to join us in exploring the drama of many periods in addition to the golden age in Elizabethan England. The policy of the Festival, from the day we started in 1972, has been to give no quarter, to take no short-cuts, in our search for excellence. We have not taken to cutting or reworking plays to build an audience by keeping back the more difficult plays or passages. We have produced *Hamlet, Richard II,* and *King Lear* uncut. We have produced one of only a handful of uncut performances of *Romeo and Juliet* produced in the past century, and by doing so shed new light on many ignored or forgotten aspects of this great tragedy. We have produced *Measure for Measure* and *Love's Labour's Lost* with the same conviction and dedication that we bring to the major tragedies and comedies.

Don Baker and Frank Taylor in the 1982 production, Red Fox/Second Hangin'.

The ASF 1982 cast of Chekhov's Uncle Vanya.

Evelyn Carol Case (left) and Michele Farr (right) in ASF's 1982 production of Twelfth Night.

Kermit Brown, Arthur Hanket, and Charles Antalosky in Twelfth Night, *1982.*

We have also produced plays from a broad cross-section of world theatre. Works by Molière, Feydeau, Ibsen, Stoppard, Coward, Barton, Machiavelli, and Wycherley, have all graced our stage.

What sets the Festival apart perhaps more than anything else is our commitment to the integrity of our authors' choices and intents. We are not, and never will be, a theatre where a director or an actor will pervert or alter the playwright's wishes. This is a theatre which always believes that our job is to serve the genius of the playwright, not impose our personal perceptions on him.

We continue to grow and continue to explore. In coming seasons I hope to present works by Chekhov, Wilde, Shaw, O'Neill, Congreve, Sheridan, Regnard, and Rostand, in addition to works by other 17th-century playwrights including Jonson, Webster, Marlowe, Beaumont, Fletcher, and Ford.

Festival Extras

The commitment to expanding into a year-round operation and putting together a company that could work in residence eluded Platt and the ASF for thirteen years. Although Festival activities and a few key staff members were noticeable throughout the year, the primary focus remained the summer Festival. Many additions and refinements gave the Festival added publicity, larger audiences, and more diversified programs. The ASF staff cultivated these areas and turned them into integral parts of the total program.

The 1978 program announced the first of these "Festival extras": a fall and winter ASF-sponsored film series was planned and included an interesting mixture of Shakespeare films and other classics, including *Citizen Kane, Anna Karenina,* and *The Magic Flute.* The 1980 program listed more numerous extras, including pre-show discussions, after-theatre meet-the-cast parties, cookie-and-tea lobby meetings, lectures, tours, and Elizabethan pageantry and church services popularly known as "Shakespeare Sundays." A concert series nicknamed "Music at St. Michael's," headquartered in a historic Anniston church, featured seventeenth- and eighteenth-century organ music, cello and piano concerts, the ASF Madrigal Singers, and a brass quintet. Announced in the same program were six classic films including Noel Coward's *Blithe Spirit* and Shakespeare's *Richard III* starring Lord Laurence Olivier.

Dr. Gertrude Luther volunteering for the ASF in Anniston.

The 1980 Season

The Alabama Shakespeare Festival had indeed developed a diverse and exciting series of programs, picnics, lectures, and concerts to supplement everyone's main reason for attending the Festival: the plays. English teachers, drama enthusiasts, and curiosity seekers from all over

Abby and Jim Ulrey preparing for the ASF summer season in Anniston.

Mary Hobbs, one of "the Ladies" in ASF's costume shop.

A film crew outside the ASF's Anniston theatre.

the United States and many foreign countries were flocking to the unlikely city of Anniston, Alabama, to experience a more settled Platt. In 1980, the Festival expanded to produce all five plays in the main theatre in repertory and officially became a League of Resident Theatres company, which according to Platt, represents "the highest level of the theatrical art in America."

The ambitious 1980 season included *Romeo and Juliet, Tartuffe, The Two Gentlemen of Verona, The Importance of Being Earnest,* and *Cymbeline.* The season was an expression of one of Platt's most important and continuing goals for the ASF: "to create an atmosphere in which technicians, costumers, staff, and actors can work comfortably as a unit and grow in their roles during the summer." Artistic quality, with an emphasis on growth and comfort is the reason that many company members continued to return to the ASF every year despite nominal pay increases and humble working conditions. In interview after interview throughout the years, company members expressed their dedication to the Alabama Shakespeare Festival and attributed their commitment to the ensemble effort, the team approach to production, the warmth and graciousness of the community, and the consistent artistic quality of the productions.

The critics responded most favorably to the 1980 season, led by R. C. Fulton of the *Shakespeare Quarterly:* "This summer the Alabama Shakespeare Festival showed how vital a function regional theatre can perform in the sustaining and enlivening of the Shakespeare Canon." According to Fulton, "There was nothing in the Shakespearean offerings

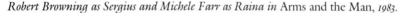

Robert Browning as Sergius and Michele Farr as Raina in Arms and the Man, *1983.*

to suggest museum renditions. What we got instead were vital, direct shows, vivid recreations."

1980 marked a change in administrative leadership as Michael Maso replaced Anne Zimmerman as Managing Director of the Alabama Shakespeare Festival. The administrative and artistic team of Martin L. Platt, Josephine Ayers (Executive Producer and Board Chairman), and Michael Maso committed itself to setting the artistic standard for the South and boosted the ASF budget to over one-half million dollars for the first time in the Festival's history. The 1980 Acting Conservatory, under the direction of Anne Sandoe, also continued to grow during this period. The fall tour of *The Two Gentlemen of Verona* marked the ASF's first commitment to touring at the same level of production as the summer season in an effort to reach out to the entire Southeast.

The Second Decade

In 1981, the ASF once again ventured into new artistic territory, using Atlanta as a pre-Anniston performance base for a rousing production of the musical, *Oh, Coward!* which later opened the ASF's newly acquired second theatre in the heart of downtown Anniston. The addition of a second performance space for the ASF allowed for more flexibility in the performance schedule, added variety to the season selection, and facilitated additional casting possibilities for the Artistic Director. Dubbed "the ACT Theatre," the second stage offered seating for only 100 patrons; it provided a more intimate atmosphere and a much sought-after alternative to the main theatre's 1,000-seat house.

Oh Coward! ran for nearly fifty performances at the ACT Theatre, while *A Midsummer Night's Dream, Henry IV, Part I, Much Ado About Nothing,* and *The Servant of Two Masters* kept the main stage busy with as many as nine performances a week over a five-week period. The Festival's tenth anniversary was hailed statewide as an important event in Alabama. Governor Fob James recognized the Festival for having "brought great drama, comedy, and professionalism to the people of Alabama, and regional and national recognition of the quality of the cultural life of our state."

In an effort to combat financial problems and provide for the future, a "Second Decade" campaign to raise funds for the Alabama Shakespeare Festival was launched in coordination with the 1981 season. The Festival's financial difficulties largely stemmed from the rapid professional growth of the company, the local financial support base, and the inability to amortize expenses during the short summer seasons. The

Betty Leighton and Michele Farr in the 1982 hit, All's Well That Ends Well.

short season was dictated by the schedule of the ASF's theatre, which doubled as an educational complex in the fall, winter, and spring.

The Festival's tenth anniversary seemed to signal a time of evaluation and retrospection for all members of the ASF community, and Platt was compelled to share a few of his thoughts with the Festival audience:

> It seems only yesterday that we were rehearsing and performing—and sweltering—in the old high school, with motorcycles zooming past the open doors during the graveyard scene in *Hamlet!*
>
> Looking back on the first ten years of The Festival, I have many pleasant memories, and, yes, a few painful ones, too. No youngster ever grows up without a few stumbles. For me, and for the theatre, these have been an exciting and rewarding ten years. There has been great joy in watching the theatre grow and flourish, gaining stature, developing our conservatory programs, adding the touring seasons.
>
> As I travel around the country visiting other theatres, I am always gratified to learn that the Festival is known and respected by the other professionals in our field. The theatre is an exciting and extraordinary place. The work we do is transitory and illusory. One night's performance cannot be re-created; the chemistry between audience and players is a rare and special thing—the exclusive province of the theatre.

The 1981 season was indeed a happy season artistically. A review in *Shakespeare Quarterly* summed up the feelings many reviewers had for the Festival:

> I hope the Alabama Shakespeare Festival can keep it up. This lively professional group has attracted audiences to Anniston from all over the Southeast. In an area more associated with the Talladega 500 and the Crimson Tide than with first-rate classical theatre, Alabama Shakespeare Festival is a phenomenon to be cherished.

The ASF "phenomenon" continued to lead to increased regional and national attention. In a letter to President and Mrs. Jimmy Carter, *Anniston Star* editor H. Brandt Ayers invited the Carters to the Alabama Shakespeare Festival to celebrate the "tenth birthday of what seemed to be a preposterous idea—live professional classical theatre in a small town in the Deep South." More and more, the national press, radio, and television stations expressed their interest and surprise at the longevity of the ASF and the quality and integrity of the productions.

Deficit Dilemmas

Unfortunately, local and regional associates of the Festival were less enamored with the ASF's financial and organizational management.

Audience members in the Anniston theatre lobby in 1983.

Presenting a medley of hits from the 1982 ASF season (clockwise from top):
Romeo and Juliet, *with John Heider and Evelyn Carol Case.*

Uncle Vanya, *with Linda Stephens, Michele Farr, Billie Brenan, and Frank Raiter;*

Twelfth Night, *with Evelyn Carol Case, Charles Antalosky, and Michael McKenzie;*

Cal Winn and Michael McKenzie in the ASF's controversial The Taming of the Shrew *in 1983.*

Major deficits over a two-year period, a lukewarm response to the Board of Directors' Second Decade fund-raising program, and the failure of two major fund-raising ventures resulted in an accumulated deficit of over a quarter of a million dollars. These problems seriously jeopardized the ASF's 1982 season, and only a last-minute reprieve by Alabama businessman Winton M. Blount saved the Festival from almost certain extinction.

Intensive informational meetings and negotiations with the ASF Board of Directors revealed a two-fold financial problem. The first concern was a major deficit that was still in excess of $130,000. The second long-range problem was the Festival's seeming inability to survive as a professional classical repertory theatre without a permanent theatre available on a full-time basis.

Based on these findings, Winton M. "Red" and Carolyn Blount proposed to contribute $130,000 to virtually eliminate the Festival's past debts. They also proposed to build the ASF a new home in Montgomery—Alabama's state capital—if the ASF Board of Directors and staff were willing to move the base of operations.

A Festival in Transition

As discussed earlier, the Alabama Shakespeare Festival's inability to cope with its ever-rising expenses was directly tied to the performance season, historically limited to only four to six weeks due to other uses of the Anniston theatre. It seemed clear to the Board of Directors, and to businessman Winton M. Blount, that retiring the $130,000 accumulated deficit to avoid bankruptcy would solve half the problem and building the ASF a new home of its own would solve the remaining half of the problem.

Media reactions to the Blount/ASF agreement were plentiful and mixed. *The Huntsville Times* wrote, "Although we would hate to see the Shakespeare Festival leave its native city of Anniston . . . such a move may be necessary for the Festival to survive at all." *The Anniston Star*'s editorial team concluded, "For Annistonians, it is not the happiest moment in the world, contemplating a Montgomery-centered Alabama Shakespeare Festival, until one gets to the ultimate meaning: it assures the survival of something created, worked for, and enjoyed for more than a decade."

The Montgomery-based *Alabama Journal* commented that "devotees of the theatre are justifiably pleased at the prospect of the acclaimed Alabama Shakespeare Festival being moved to Montgomery, where magnate Winton Blount has offered to build a performing arts center to house it."

After reviewing all of the options, the Alabama Shakespeare Festival Board of Directors and staff endorsed the following plan, thus ensuring the future of the Festival and embarking on a new course for the State Theatre:

WHEREAS, ASF, a non-profit association, has been based in Anniston, Alabama, for the last ten years and has provided fine classical theatre productions in the summer in Anniston and other cities in this region; and

WHEREAS, ASF wishes to expand the scope of the Festival in this region and reach more people in longer seasons; and

WHEREAS, this objective can best be achieved if a permanent performing arts center is available in a city larger than Anniston so that the Festival could have a permanent home theatre and operate for a longer season; and

WHEREAS, Blount, himself or through others, plans to build a performing arts center in Montgomery, Alabama, appropriately designed for Shakespearean productions, which could serve as a permanent home for ASF; and

WHEREAS, such a home theatre could be used as a base on which to develop support for the continued operation and funding for ASF; and

WHEREAS, it is deemed appropriate that ASF, The State Theatre of Alabama, be located in the state capitol . . . ASF will transfer its home base of operations to Montgomery, Alabama, effective January 1, 1985, or as soon as the proposed performing arts center is completed, whichever is later.

An editorial in a later Montgomery paper explained part of the background on the Festival's move and summarized the general reaction of the Montgomery business community:

The Alabama Shakespeare Festival is coming to the capital from Anniston, where it began 12 years ago. It grew into an artistic success and drew national praise. But financing it proved too much for its patrons there and Montgomery developer Winton M. "Red" Blount arranged to relocate it to Montgomery and build it a theatre on his estate . . . it is indeed a large purpose, a grand one. It will bring distinction to Montgomery and to the state, drawing an even larger audience with its new quarters and expanded season. The thought of this new asset brings on the keenest of pleasant expectations.

An important part of the "Blount Guaranty" is the agreement that the Alabama Shakespeare Festival Board of Directors "will continue to operate during the summer seasons of 1982, 1983, and 1984 from its base in Anniston," and this guaranty enabled the Festival to charge into 1982, 1983, and 1984 with renewed vigor and promise.

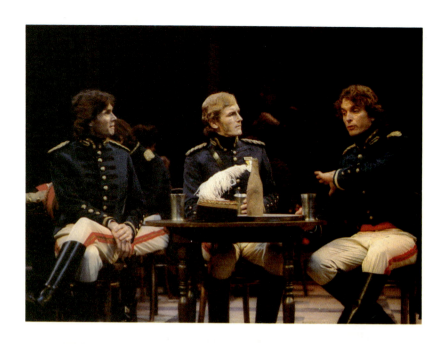

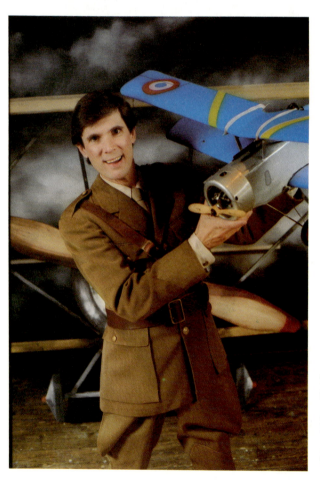

Top: Robert Browning, Bruce Cromer, and Michael McKenzie in the 1983 production of All's Well That Ends Well.

Robert Browning in the title role of the Canadian musical, Billy Bishop Goes to War, *1983.*

Bruce Cromer and Carol Allin in ASF's 1983 comedy, The Taming of the Shrew.

Left: Frank Raiter as Father Tim in Mass Appeal, *1983.*

Below, right: John-Frederick Jones and Lilene Mansell as Petruchio and Kate in the 1983 ASF version of The Taming of the Shrew.

Below, left: A box office customer in the ASF lobby in Anniston.

The Making of a Regional Theatre   57

The Final Years in Anniston

Featuring *Hamlet, Uncle Vanya,* and *Twelfth Night* in the "Festival Theatre," and a "mini-festival of Southern Folk Theatre" at the ACT Playhouse, the Festival continued to build new audiences and promote classical theatre in Anniston in 1982. *Red Fox/ Second Hangin'* performed by the Roadside Theatre and *Junebug Jabbo Jones,* produced by the Free Southern Theatre, were booked into the ACT Theatre, marking the first time the Festival offered outside productions as part of its subscription package. Rounding out the 1982 Festival package were a conservatory production of *The Comedy of Errors,* two Elizabethan church services, pre-show discussions, after-theatre discussions, meet-the-cast parties, an opening night gala, a 5,000-meter run (appropriately nicknamed "A Midsummer Morn's Run"), and organ, chamber music, early choral and violin-viola duo concerts.

Although the ASF trimmed its season to only three major productions in 1982, the critics and audience continued to embrace the company and applaud the efforts of the artists. Montgomery newspaper reviewer Fred Lippincott reported that the "Shakespeare troupe has never been better, in fact the best this reviewer has seen in a half dozen seasons of theatregoing at Anniston." A local radio station critic cited the 1982 production of *Twelfth Night* as "the brightest thing to grace the Festival Theatre in Anniston," and the *Atlanta Constitution* critic's "pick of the plays" was Chekhov's *Uncle Vanya.* A successful fall tour of *Romeo and Juliet* through eight southeastern states rounded out the 1982 season.

Later in 1982, in preparation for the expansion, Artistic Director Martin L. Platt, Architect Thomas A. Blount, and Executive Producer Josephine Ayers joined Carolyn and Winton M. Blount and others in a research expedition exploring theatres throughout America. This research trip was designed to introduce the planning team to buildings, designs, programs, productions, and theories of model professional theatre operations in North America. As part of the cross-country tours, the group visited the Guthrie Theatre in Minnesota, the Old Globe Theatre in California, the Denver Center Theatre in Colorado, the Shaw Festival in Canada, the Mark Taper Forum in California, the Minneapolis Children's Theatre in Minnesota, the South Coast Repertory Theatre in California, and Canada's Stratford Festival.

At the same time the key architectural plans were being discussed, the ASF Board of Directors were actively searching for a new chief executive officer to fill the void that was left by Managing Director Michael Maso, who resigned in October 1982, and Executive Producer Josephine Ayers, who announced her intention to step down effective January 1983.

Jim Volz, a theatre manager teaching at the University of Colorado in Boulder, visited the ASF in the summer of 1982; he took over the administrative reigns of the theatre later that year. Soon thereafter, John E. Kelly, a longtime Board supporter and Anniston businessman, was elected Chairman of the Board of Directors. This new executive team joined Martin L. Platt in preparing for the 1983 season, expanding the base of operations, improving all financial controls, and beginning the crucial transition from seasonal operations to year-round regional theatre status.

Artistically and financially, the 1983 season of *All's Well That Ends Well, The Taming of the Shrew, Arms and the Man, King Lear,* and *Mass Appeal* will be remembered as one of the highlights of the Festival's thirteen years in Anniston.

According to Platt, "The 1983 season simply fell into place as one of the most well-balanced, artistically diverse, and theatrically exciting seasons that we have produced." The theatre critics seemed to agree. Kenneth Shorey, a longtime ASF critic from *The Birmingham News,* called the season "a whopping success." Shorey maintained that "this

Cast members of All's Well That Ends Well, *1983.*

Mayor Folmar, Governor Wallace, and Mr. and Mrs. Blount break ground for the new ASF complex in Montgomery in August 1983.

Construction workers on the new theatre work around the clock to assure the December 1985 opening.

The fast track construction of the new complex begins, featuring designs by Blount/Pittman and Associates.

Artistic Director Martin L. Platt and Managing Director Jim Volz outside the nearly completed ASF complex in Montgomery.

Mrs. Folmar, Mrs. Richards, Lt. General Richards and Mayor Folmar parade ASF costumes in an Elizabethan fund-raiser at the Governor's House in Montgomery.

summer offers a literate, wise, compassionate, funny/serious, thoroughly excellent production of Bill C. Davis's *Mass Appeal;* a fully believable humanistic *King Lear;* a joyously knowing, elegantly mannered *All's Well That Ends Well,* with laughter, tears, high comedy and low; and now a gay, light-hearted staging of Shaw's *Arms and the Man* like a comic operetta without the music."

Helen C. Smith, theatre critic for *The Atlanta Constitution,* wrote that, "a hilarious *Shrew,* a moving *Lear,* an archly comic Shaw and the southern premiere of the Broadway hit *Mass Appeal* are the plums of the 12th annual Alabama Shakespeare Festival. . . . it is the best balanced and most rewarding festival ever staged here." Richard L. Coe of *The Washington Post* wrote, "What a marvelously varied feast is this 12th Alabama Shakespeare Festival! These five productions of obvious professional skills have something for everyone. . . . the ASF is proving itself to be in at least the upper quarter of American regional theatres."

Although the Festival's controversial World War II version of *The Taming of the Shrew* raised the ire of a few patrons and critics, the majority of the reviews and patron surveys revealed an overriding excitement and satisfaction regarding the ASF's artistic product. The artistic success of the plays also helped the theatre financially as the season enabled the ASF to break the string of four major deficit years in a row. Contributions rose 108 percent and box office income rose 23 percent, allowing the Festival to carry a surplus into the 1984 fiscal year.

While audiences were attending 1983 performances, the ASF staff and Board of Directors were monitoring ongoing operations and conducting long-range planning sessions for the Montgomery opening. Marketing efforts were significantly increased in 1983 and 1984 in hopes that the increased visibility and public relations endeavors would pay off during the ASF's expansion. One of the most important marketing tools was the display throughout Alabama of a model of the new ASF complex and grounds.

A special educational project created by a partnership between the Committee for the Humanities in Alabama and the ASF sparked statewide enthusiasm regarding the literary merits and production joys of Shakespeare. The project, entitled "Shakespeare: Theatre in the Mind" was funded by the National Endowment for the Humanities and resulted in Shakespeare seminars, films, displays, and library materials being disseminated and integrated into more than eighteen separate communities in Alabama. As the final part of the seminar in each community, participants visited the 1984 Alabama Shakespeare Festival and discussed the productions.

In 1984, the ASF produced *Love's Labour's Lost, Macbeth, She Stoops to Conquer, Billy Bishop Goes to War,* and *Oh, Mr. Faulkner, Do You Write?* A theatrical high point during the season was BBC Shakespeare Series

Producer Jonathan Miller's visit to the ASF and subsequent reference to the "fine work of the company." Area critics were much more enthusiastic. Kenneth Shorey of *The Birmingham News* hailed *Macbeth* as "quite simply the best, most brilliantly conceived and executed production I've ever seen, and I've seen *Macbeth* produced more often than any other Shakespeare play." Sam Hodges of *The Birmingham Post-Herald* agreed, calling *Macbeth* "a must-see, a knockout, the Festival's best production of a tragedy in recent years." *The Atlanta Constitution*'s Linda Sherbert labeled the ASF "the South's leading professional classical theatre" and described *Macbeth, Love's Labour's Lost,* and *Billy Bishop Goes to War* as "all winners." *She Stoops to Conquer* and *Oh, Mr. Faulkner, Do You Write?* were also heralded by the regional media. *The Birmingham News* applauded the "rich, colorful staging" of *She Stoops to Conquer,* and *The Montgomery Advertiser* applauded John Maxwell's Faulkner as being "too brief because we love the visit."

Jonathan Miller, BBC Shakespeare, ASF guest speaker, 1984.

Perhaps as important as the critics' comments were the many key developments in the Festival's administrative structure and resources. For the first time in the Festival's history, a full-time Director of Marketing (Jay Drury), Business Manager (Doug Perry), and Production Manager (Mark Loigman) were added to the administrative staff to assist in the 1984 season, prepare for the 1985 move, and plan for future operations in Montgomery. As part of the ASF's planning process, key members of the Montgomery community were invited to join important members of the ASF Board of Directors to form a new steering team labeled "the ASF Transition Committee." These crucial team members were charged with assisting in a smooth transition of the base of the ASF operations from Anniston to Montgomery and provided advice, guidance, and important background and information to the ASF staff. They also paved the way for a healthy exchange of ideas between Anniston's experienced and enthusiastic volunteer workers and many potential volunteers in Montgomery. Members of the ASF Guild in Anniston even traveled the tedious two-hour, two-lane road to Montgomery to share their experiences, successes, and suggestions with their interested counterparts in Montgomery.

From 1972 to 1984, the audience for the Alabama Shakespeare Festival increased from the 3,000 brave individuals who first ventured into the unair-conditioned Anniston High School to nearly 70,000 Shakespeare fans from throughout the United States and many foreign countries. The artistic journey of the Alabama Shakespeare Festival contains many challenges, examples, and lessons for individuals interested in the overall process and decision-making of theatre personnel. The following chapters will spotlight crucial decisions and moments of history in the making of North America's newest year-round regional theatre, the Alabama Shakespeare Festival.

John-Frederick Jones as Claudius and Bruce Cromer in the title role of the ASF's 1982 Hamlet.

64   Shakespeare Never Slept Here

II

Audience Development: Shakespeare in the South?

The key to survival for any performing arts institution centers on its ability to attract audiences and the accompanying funding for support of the programs and general operations. Marketing of the arts is based on a voluntary exchange of resources, and the Alabama Shakespeare Festival's offer to trade classical repertory theatre for audiences and community financial support took years to nurture and develop.

It seems safe to say that marketing principles and basic audience development techniques took a back seat to the unbridled enthusiasm for Shakespeare and the creative work of the theatre in the early years of the Alabama Shakespeare Festival.

In 1972, audience development efforts focused more on publicity than on any other marketing tool. Flyers, newspaper articles, and word-of-mouth publicity comprised the bulk of the campaign the first year. "As the founder of the theatre, the first year's marketing was up to me, and the expense and effort was minimal," explains Artistic Director Platt. Festival volunteers pieced together a mailing list that targeted prospective audience members in Anniston, while other volunteers concentrated on collecting the key mailing lists and prime zip codes in Birmingham. For the most part, the audience development campaign and publicity worked within a thirty-mile radius of Anniston, but little effort was made to appeal to the larger surrounding cities of Atlanta, Chattanooga, Mobile, or Montgomery. An Anniston businessman, Donald Goodman, assisted with the first year of the campaign and contributed most of the public relations and design ideas for 1972. A small

Michele Farr and Bruce Cromer as Helena and Bertram in All's Well That Ends Well, *1983.*

group of volunteers, including members of the acting company, helped distribute information, and less than twenty area businesses assisted in advertising.

Prior to the ASF's opening in 1972, the area's primary summer entertainment included fishing, boating, and the annual stock car race in the neighboring city of Talladega. As the only Shakespeare festival and virtually the only classical theatre between Dallas and Washington, D.C., the ASF didn't face a great deal of competition and helped fill a void that had long been empty. However, at the same time, the Alabama Shakespeare Festival was facing area resistance to Shakespeare either through ignorance of who the playwright was, or reticence to attend the play of a writer who had bored them in high school English classes.

Although the first season drew over 3,000 people to the two Shakespeare comedies (*Two Gentlemen of Verona* and *The Comedy of Errors*) and Ibsen's *Hedda Gabler,* the Alabama Shakespeare Festival felt that they could only count on 300–400 regular Anniston playgoers. "At first," explains Platt, "we were operating under the naive assumption that people everywhere else in the country responded well to Shakespeare and that people in the Deep South would too. All of our mailings were based on upper middle-class people who traditionally go to the theatre. Although it was easy getting coverage in town, it was difficult getting people to take the ASF seriously."

Betty Leighton, Michele Farr, and Bruce Cromer in All's Well That Ends Well, *1983.*

In 1972, ticket prices were set at $5 for the three-play subscriptions, and $2 for single tickets. "We were trying to stay competitive with the community theatre tickets and stay in the same ball park as movies and other entertainment options," reasoned Platt. In 1972, only $1,500 was spent in total on administrative expenses and only a small portion of that was spent on publicity and audience development. Additional services were donated, but the overall personnel and budget commitment to audience development was minimal.

AUDIENCE STATISTICS

YEAR	SUMMER SEASON AUDIENCES	TOURING AUDIENCES
1972	3,000	
1973	5,000	
1974	7,000	
1975	10,000	
1976	10,000	
1977	15,000	
1978	23,000	22,000
1979	24,000	40,000
1980	25,000	40,000
1981	26,000	25,000
1982	21,400	33,000
1983	23,400	33,000
1984	25,500	36,000

"The actors are at hand and by their show, You shall know all that you are like to know."

A MIDSUMMER NIGHT'S DREAM

In order to boost their audience size and survive financially, the Alabama Shakespeare Festival Board of Directors realized that they would have to market the Festival to a greater extent in Birmingham, which was sixty miles to the west, and in Atlanta, which was ninety miles

Arthur Hanket in a mafioso version of Goldoni's The Servant of Two Masters.

to the east. These two areas were targeted as primary audience sources, and a small effort was also undertaken to spread the word of the Festival's existence through as much of the Southeast as possible. Although enthusiasm was high following the first season, Anniston's general population wasn't accustomed to Shakespeare or regular theatregoing.

However, the individuals who saw the local advertising campaign and came to the plays in 1972 developed into an excellent volunteer resource in 1973. On August 1, 1973, the Alabama Shakespeare Festival Guild was officially founded for this express purpose: (as stated in their constitution) "to stimulate interest in the Alabama Shakespeare Festival, and, whenever possible to furnish volunteer help when requested by the ASF Board of Directors."

In 1973, a manifesto detailing the Festival's goals helped clarify the Board of Directors and the ASF staff's intent to broaden the audience base of the theatre. As stated in the minutes of the Board of Directors' notes in 1973:

> The Festival's goals are: a) to produce professional productions of the plays of Shakespeare and other great playwrights during the summer for the people of the Southeast; b) to present the plays in a manner which will appeal to *all* audiences (i.e., to prove to audiences that Shakespeare was above all an entertaining playwright speaking to people of all times); c) to cause an awareness not only in the Southeast but also throughout the nation that there is a cultural awakening taking place in the South; d) to bring people from the Southeast and the nation together in Anniston each summer to enjoy the plays of the greatest playwrights of the world produced professionally in the beautiful surroundings of the southeastern United States.

With these guidelines in hand, the Alabama Shakespeare Festival volunteers, a skeletal staff, and the Board of Directors printed the Festival's first real season brochure listing single ticket prices at $3 for adults and $2 for students. Subscriptions to all four of the 1973 plays were only $10 for adults and $6.50 for students. The key slogan selected for 1973 advertising was "SHAKESPEARE LIVES IN ALABAMA: TO ENTERTAIN THE ENTIRE FAMILY."

In a 1973 program note, Platt asserts that the Alabama Shakespeare Festival "has gained the respect of theatre people throughout the United States. They know we are doing for the South what Stratford, Connecticut, and Ashland, Oregon, have done for their regions." Although Platt may have been overly optimistic, the Board of Directors picked up on this enthusiasm and appealed to the city and state by announcing that "Serving not only Anniston, but all of Alabama and the Southeast, the Festival is helping to put Anniston on the map and boost area prestige and tourism." According to an article in a Pensacola, Florida, newspaper, the Alabama Shakespeare Festival was succeeding in appealing to audiences throughout the Southeast. "Platt succeeded in his intention to illuminate the text and make it more accessible and delightful to audiences. Advertising now reaches five states, each of which was represented by license plates in the parking lot." Although the paper's reviewer maintained that "the Southeast's first Shakespearean Festival seems oddly waylaid in Anniston's pastoral remoteness," it is one of the first out-of-state papers to recognize that "Anniston also holds the distinction of breathing life into the literary Shakespeare: returning him as a man of the living theatre for summer visitors in bermuda shorts and hand-laced sandals to relish."

In 1974, a direct-mail campaign (coordinated by William Acker) to approximately 40,000 people in Atlanta, Birmingham, Gadsden, and Talladega helped secure an audience. And 1974 is labeled by most Alabama Shakespeare Festival enthusiasts as a breakthrough year artistically as production values and newspaper reviews both seemed to take a positive turn. *A Midsummer Night's Dream, Romeo and Juliet, The Taming of the Shrew,* and *The School for Wives* were all received well, and according to Thomas Noland, "It was 1974's lavish, brilliant, *A Midsummer Night's Dream* which changed the tone of newspaper reviews from condescending approval to genuine admiration, and which, more importantly, demonstrated the real value of the trial and error that had gone before."

The push for more regional recognition, publicity, and direct-mail audience development pieces continued throughout the mid-1970s as the Alabama Shakespeare Festival audiences steadily grew and peaked at around 10,000 people in 1975 and 1976. Volunteers Glenda Knight and Terry Eaton were instrumental in public relations, publications, and audience development, although the Artistic Director and Board President still assumed the heaviest burden of responsibility. In fact, Platt remained heavily involved in all of ASF's management and audience development concerns until Anne Zimmerman's appointment in 1977 as the ASF's first full-time management professional. The period from 1977 to 1979 marked the first time the ASF had a professional to coordinate all aspects of the audience development campaign. The investment paid off. Audiences jumped from 10,000 to 15,000 to 20,000 in the late 1970s, largely due to the organizational planning directed by Anne Zimmerman and the audience development and marketing consultation provided by the Foundation for the Extension and Development of the American Professional Theatre (FEDAPT).

"The gods are above; time must friend or end."

TROILUS AND CRESSIDA

Kermit Brown and Evelyn Carol Case in Arms and the Man, *1983.*

Shakespeare Never Slept Here

Frederic B. Vogel, Executive Director of FEDAPT, explained that FEDAPT accepted the Alabama Shakespeare Festival's request for management technical assistance in the beginning of 1977. According to Vogel, "Management Technical Assistance was offered to help develop the management structure as the Festival's first step toward developing into a fully professional theatre." FEDAPT supplied a wide range of consultants to the Festival, including management personnel from the Guthrie Theatre in Minneapolis and the McCarter Theatre in New Jersey. Vogel asserts that "it was during this time the Festival developed a base for its management staff and was able to present a sophisticated marketing image to its audiences."

In a follow-up letter of January 18, 1977, Vogel wrote Managing Director Anne Zimmerman and earmarked audience development as the Festival's number one priority at this stage of the theatre's development. He pinpointed the ASF's major problem in this area when he wrote:

> Quite simply, since everything has been done administratively by volunteers, there is not the long-range planning accomplished by step-by-step supervision and follow-through that full-time professionals can guarantee.

The arrival of Anne Zimmerman and the consultation with FEDAPT produced immediate changes in the ASF's audience development program and resulted in restructured single ticket prices, a new season ticket concept, increased group sales efforts, and the development of a

Charles Antalosky in King Lear, *1983.*

Catherine Moore and Evelyn Carol Case consoling each other for wearing the wrong costumes in a photo call for The Comedy Of Errors, *1983.*

Cast members in an updated ASF version of Macbeth *in 1984.*

Michele Farr as Helena in the 1983 ASF production of
All's Well That Ends Well.

72   Shakespeare Never Slept Here

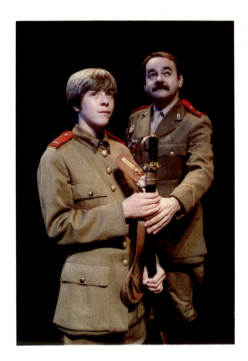

Douglas Stewart as Fleance and Charles Antalosky as Banquo in the 1984 production of Macbeth.

A. D. Cover, Lisa McMillan, Jack Wetherall, and Robert Browning in the ASF 1984 tragedy, Macbeth.

campaign with an emphasis on Alabama's tourism potential in relation to the Festival. These changes not only resulted in much larger audiences, but they ignited interest and exposure on a regional and national basis while boosting earned income from $43,328 in 1976 to all-time highs of $72,946 in 1977; $186,901 in 1978; and $271,703 in 1979. By its 1979 season, the ASF was pulling in 24,000 patrons from all over the Southeast with wide representation from throughout the United States and many foreign countries. The upward trend continued with 25,000 patrons in 1980 and 26,000 in 1981.

Alabama Shakespeare Festival records, statistics, and interviews with key personnel all seem to indicate an evolutionary discovery process in the early years of the Festival (1972–75). Although the Artistic Director and various Board members made efforts to articulate current goals and long-range plans, a coherent, well-researched audience development strategy eluded the Festival staff for a number of years. After the first year's offerings, it was clear that an audience base outside Anniston was going to be crucial if the Festival planned to grow and survive. Efforts to tap into regional arts audiences tended to center on enthusiastic spurts producing instant results or failures, rather than ongoing audience development techniques that would build a strong audience on a continuing basis. For example, when funding permitted, the Alabama Shakespeare Festival drew on key Birmingham zip codes for a direct mail campaign and spread brochures in other potential audience centers. However, the efforts tended to be one time "hit or

Evelyn Carol Case and Kermit Brown (above); and A. D. Cover, Michele Farr, Robert Browning, and Betty Leighton (right) in ASF's 1983 production of Arms and the Man.

74

Left and below: Michele Farr and James Donadio in the Alabama Shakespeare festival's 1983 production of Arms and the Man.

Above: A. D. Cover, Betty Leighton, and Robert Browning in Shaw's Arms and the Man *at ASF in 1983.*

Right: Robert Miller II and Michael McKenzie in the 1982 ASF production of Romeo and Juliet.

miss" mailings as opposed to a carefully coordinated media campaign of newsletters, brochures, and perhaps telephone or personal contacts.

A 1977 FEDAPT publication focusing on audience development stresses the importance of identifying and defining the theatre's past, present, and potential market:

> Whom do you want to reach? What do they want? What is their profile (geographical location, economic level, etc.)? Who else is in that market? Have they been surveyed? By what means? Have you analyzed the results? What other advertising is in that market? Do you know how to "test" your market for pricing? for copy?

According to Joseph Melillo, Former Director of Field Services for FEDAPT:

> The people who come to your theatre, as well as those who do not, have an impression of your theatre. The impression is composed of many elements which you can control. You want to control these components in order to build an image or impression which corresponds to your objectives and self-definition. This allows you to zero in on your market.

For the first few years of the Alabama Shakespeare Festival, little effort was made to define and zero in on what would become the Festival's primary market. Festival personnel had little control over their audience's perceived image largely because they were still struggling to define the nature of the theatre they had created.

A. D. Cover as Gloucester in the 1983 production of King Lear.

Even in the early years, Platt articulated and maintained his vision of competing with the other North American Shakespeare festivals. However, due to budget and personnel restraints, the marketing efforts and key audience development publications were far from professional quality and generally only caught the attention of interested community members and their curious friends from neighboring cities. Slowly, the theatre's reputation for unique and high-quality productions spread into the regional centers of Birmingham, Chattanooga, and Atlanta, and by 1975, word of mouth and clearer sales brochures assisted the ASF's audience development endeavors by building a core of approximately 10,000 patrons.

The budgets throughout the early 1970s reveal a nominal commitment to widespread advertising and publicity even when one considers that many services and products were donated. From 1972 to 1975, the total commitment to publicity, promotions, audience development, and advertising ranged from around $500 in 1972 and 1975 to around $2,000 in 1973 and 1974. The key audience development tool for each of these campaigns was the season brochure, and for three years this simply consisted of a brown, seven-by-eleven-inch flyer with drab photographs, graphics, and hand lettering mixed with typeset copy. In

Arthur Hanket as the young priest and Frank Raiter as Father Tim in ASF's 1983 production of Bill C. Davis's Mass Appeal.

1975, a clearer, two-color brochure improved the direct-mail barrage and offered a simple theme; "SHAKESPEARE LIVES IN ALABAMA." Evidently, the brochure worked so well in 1975 that the ASF repeated the exact same color, format, size, design, and slogan in 1976.

Discussing these early audience development campaigns seems somewhat difficult for Platt, who uneasily recalls that "for the first five years the Alabama Shakespeare Festival had no professional management— and for two of the first five years the budget was made without a manager!" According to Platt, "When Anne Zimmerman took charge in 1977, it was the first time we had someone to coordinate the total campaign and it really worked. FEDAPT helped us with consultants and marketing advice and outlined with us what we should be doing and what we weren't doing."

The Festival made major audience development strides under Zimmerman's leadership as her overall marketing strategy included making season tickets more attractive to potential patrons, focusing on the "tourism angle" by contacting local and regional motels, hotels, restaurants, and libraries, and targeting twelve specific cities: Anniston, Birmingham, Huntsville, Gadsden, Jacksonville, Talladega, Montgomery, Tuscaloosa, and Auburn in Alabama; Rome and Atlanta, Georgia; and Chattanooga, Tennessee. Zimmerman also presented her plan to "include reasonable budgets for administration, promotion, and sales," and to organize more attractive brochures, newsletters, and publications in general.

As mentioned earlier in this chapter, these efforts and the year-long planning and follow-through orchestrated by Anne Zimmerman and administrative assistant Glenda Knight paid off with major increases in attendance in 1978 and 1979. In 1978, the ASF began mailing two separate brochures for the first time; one brochure focused on season subscription sales, and the second brochure centered on single ticket sales. The brochures were the backbone of what Platt calls the "ugliest but

Arthur Hanket as the young priest in Bill C. Davis's Mass Appeal, *1983.*

Bruce Cromer, A. D. Cover, and Andrew Barnicle in the 1984 comedy, She Stoops to Conquer.

A. D. Cover and Charles Antalosky in the 1983 production of King Lear.

most successful campaign in the Festival's history." The orange, purple, and green brochure package featured a clear and clever look at the plays and special features of Anniston and the Alabama Shakespeare Festival. It sold over 20,000 tickets.

The Festival's massive increase in audience numbers couldn't have happened without an equally significant increase in budget support for publicity, promotions, audience development, advertising, and printing. In 1979 the Festival's budget for these items increased from $27,000 in 1978 to over $42,000. The next year the budget jumped once more to over $65,000, and with this increased budget support, the Alabama Shakespeare Festival was able to reach out to a wider market area, saturate prime neighborhood targets, and sustain an ongoing campaign during the peak marketing time for the summer season.

The budget developments assisted in staff development, and Patricia Lavender, Director of Public Relations, was added to the ASF in the late 1970s. In a 1978 memo to the ASF Board of Directors, Board Chairman Josephine E. Ayers explained that:

> From these (1977 budget) figures and a study of the proposed budget for 1978, you can see that the Alabama Shakespeare Festival is not a community theatre and cannot be run on the same principle as a community theatre in any way. In addition, many of the volunteer and in-kind services we have enjoyed over the years are no longer available to us, and we must find ways to fill those gaps. While several things have been handled by volunteers in the past, they have gotten so complicated that they have to be shifted to the professional staff.

The Director of Public Relations in the late 1970s was basically responsible for all publications, graphics, photography, marketing, audience development, promotions, publicity, and record keeping as well as press relations.

Support staff for audience development increased in leaps and bounds in preparation for year-round operations, and by the mid-1980s, the one-person public relations staff had grown into a team including a Director of Marketing, Public Relations Coordinator, Volunteer Services Coordinator, Photographer, Group Sales Manager, Director of Educational Services, Telemarketing Manager, Box Office Manager, Subscriptions Manager, and various assistants.

The artistic promise and success of the Festival, combined with the community and the southeastern region's pride in establishing a professional classical repertory theatre, prompted the media to react favorably to both the Alabama Shakespeare Festival as a cultural institution and individual productions as exciting theatre comparable to the best of the nation's theatres. The print media's coverage of the Alabama Shakespeare Festival has been extremely supportive, and large amounts of space have been devoted to the Festival throughout the region.

In a similar vein, the region's radio and television stations devoted considerable space to the Festival, freely running public service announcements and often creating personal features to inform their viewers and publicize the offerings of the Alabama Shakespeare Festival. Local radio stations historically review each of the new productions the week after the plays open, and the local television stations usually follow suit.

This major media support, which includes hundreds of free inches of newspaper copy and pictures in newspapers and magazines annually, has helped offset the Festival's inability to buy ongoing ads in the region's papers and helped the Festival to build audiences through the 1970s and into the 1980s.

Perhaps the ASF's strongest audience development tool for the past decade has been the annual touring program, which has traveled thousands of miles in ten states and seventy-seven cities, under the leadership of Carol Ogus, Director of Educational Services. Festival performances have reached over a quarter of a million patrons on tour and hundreds of thousands more in its home theatres. There is no doubt that the Festival's best audience development tool is the recommendation of its most important persons—the ASF audience members.

Genevieve Mallory volunteers long hours in ASF's costume shop.

Quotable Quotes

"I expected Southern Fried Shakespeare, but your company from Alabama is the best!"—Audience member, Clearwater, Florida.

"The word has spread. When ASF hits town, run and buy your ticket. Last night's performance was almost sold out, and so is tonight's."—*Chattanooga News-Free Press,* Chattanooga, Tennessee.

"Some companies perform great plays as if they are dealing with something quite rich, yet quite dead. When presented by ASF, the plays of Shakespeare, Shaw, Wilde, etc., are alive and vital and energy-charged. The same qualities that have made Alabama football so appealing to the masses are found in Alabama theatre, along with sensitivity, beauty, and perceptivity."—Tour sponsor, Marietta, Georgia.

"What excitement you have created in our community with your freshness and high standards of excellence. Greenville will never be the same. ASF has stolen our hearts!"—President, Greenville Arts Council, Greenville, Alabama.

"Too many superlatives become shallow, but you deserve them. You succeeded in bringing the vitality of Shakespeare to a largely uninitiated audience in such a way that they left the performance not only pleasantly surprised at having enjoyed it, but actually enthusiastic."—Chairman, Lecture Committee, Toccoa Falls College, Toccoa, Georgia.

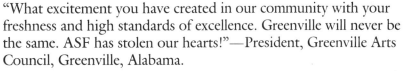

*An interior view of the Festival Stage in the
new Montgomery complex.*

III

The Backbone of the Southern Bard: The ASF Board of Directors and Key Executive Staff

How do Boards of Directors of nonprofit theatres differ from those found in commercial business? This is one of the key questions that has challenged artistic directors, managers, and board members of many professional theatres and a question that the Alabama Shakespeare Festival had to come to grips with in its formative years in the early 1970s. Although a number of individuals were interested in and supportive of the Alabama Shakespeare Festival in 1972, many were cautiously waiting to determine the viability and popularity of a southern Shakespeare Festival before formally pledging support and finances as a member of the Board of Directors. The 1972 ASF program lists the Alabama State Arts Council and the Anniston Little Theatre Board of Directors as key supporters in 1972, and the financial support and faith of these two groups helped sustain operations during the Festival's trial season. In lieu of a Board of Directors, an ASF Board of Governors was assembled with eight key regional names representing the state as an Honorary Board. At the top of this list was Mrs. George C. (Cornelia) Wallace as President of the Board.

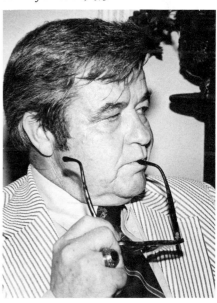

B. C. Moore, ASF's first Chairman of the Board of Directors, 1973.

It wasn't until the 1973 season that fourteen community leaders were assembled as an actual Board of Directors in preparation for the Festival's application for incorporation as a nonprofit organization. B. C. Moore, Vice-President of a major local industry, was elected the Board's first President, William P. Acker served as Vice-President, James Campbell was appointed Secretary, and Richard Byrd was the Corporation's first Treasurer.

It may come as no surprise that many of the individuals serving on the Alabama Shakespeare Festival's first Board of Directors were connected with the Anniston Community Theatre since Martin L. Platt was the Artistic Director of both organizations at the time. According to Platt, it was William P. Acker, Treasurer of the Community Theatre Board, who joined B. C. Moore in recruiting and organizing the ASF's first Board of Directors. "The first Alabama Shakespeare Festival Board was really brilliant," explained Platt. "It was perfect—attorneys, bankers, teachers, a newspaper editor, media representatives, businessmen, insurancemen, and a couple of wealthy community leaders."

According to the articles of incorporation filed on July 17, 1973, the purpose of the corporation was to produce the Alabama Shakespeare Festival annually; membership would be open to all persons or organizations interested in furthering the aims of the Alabama Shakespeare Festival. The bylaws of the corporation, established by the Board at a later date, spell out the aims and goals of the corporation and Board of Directors more clearly:

> The purpose of this corporation is to establish the Alabama Shakespeare Festival as a classical repertory theatre for the Southeast, and to promote and encourage public interest in, and support of, drama and the theatre in general.

In order to analyze and discuss the historical impact and decision making of the Board of Directors on the Alabama Shakespeare Festival, it is essential to outline the Board's own view of itself and its membership as delineated in the bylaws of the corporation. What follows is a brief summary of this 2,000-word document:

> The Board of Directors shall consist of not less than 15 nor more than 40 persons. . . . Directors shall serve for a term of three years. . . . the Board is responsible for the affairs of this corporation. Each Director shall regularly attend Board meetings, annually subscribe to the theatre, contribute to the annual fundraising effort, either personally or through solicitation, and attend all major functions of the theatre. . . . The Artistic Director and the Managing Director shall be nominated by the Executive Committee and approved by the Board of Directors. Such staff Directors shall serve at the pleasure of the Board, and the Board shall determine their compensation and other terms of employment. The Board shall be responsible for approving the annual budget, and for all major policy. The Board shall have no authority over the artistic management of the theatre other than that effected by fiscal control, and by power of appointment and dismissal of the staff Directors.

Although bylaws spell out various important elements and responsibilities of the ASF Board of Directors, it is also important to highlight

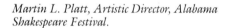

"To business that we love to rise betime, And go to't with delight."

ANTONY AND CLEOPATRA

Martin L. Platt, Artistic Director, Alabama Shakespeare Festival.

Jack Wetherall as Macbeth and Lisa McMillan as Lady Macbeth, 1984.

other characteristics of the Board in the early and mid-1970s. First and foremost, it must be understood that this Board was a working Board from the county community with little representation from outside the community. As a working Board, the members assumed virtually all of the administrative responsibilities of the theatre, including work in marketing, public relations, press relations, advertising, company management, house management, box office management, and fund-raising. Platt was contracted on a part-time seasonal basis as the guiding artistic and management force, but the implementation of key administrative tasks was largely in the hands of the volunteer Directors.

For example, in 1973, Board members sent hundreds of requests to foundations for funding, hosted parties, submitted grant requests to the City of Anniston, wrote all of Calhoun County's civic clubs, arranged for advertising, flyers, banners, and sold season subscriptions.

"If it be a man's work, I'll do it."

KING LEAR

The Backbone of the Southern Bard   87

Left: *Betty Leighton and A. D. Cover as Mrs. and Mr. Hardcastle in* She Stoops to Conquer, *1984.*

Below: *Lisa McMillan, Dawn Spare, Theresa Carver, and Drew Penick in* Love's Labour's Lost, *1984.*

Opposite: *Jack Wetherall as Berowne and Lisa McMillan as Rosaline in* Love's Labour's Lost, *1984.*

The Board also assisted in room and board arrangements for the company, housing many of them in empty beds in the local hospital and private homes.

Perhaps Josephine E. Ayers's description of the Board of Directors offers the best characterization:

> We became a Board of Directors in an odd way. It all started with pillows. Martin Platt had some friends in town for the summer and they needed pillows, among other things. So, the search was on. When the friends turned out to be actors, we knew they had to be doing something to brighten a dull summer, so we progressed from pillows to props, and a very few of us even went to that first sweltering opening night. Since then, we've sold tickets, talked on the radio, cleaned the theatre, dragged unbelievers to dozens of performances, and even whipped up a batch of hollandaise to be consumed on stage.
>
> It would be easy now to say, "We've done all we can." But the ASF Board has a history of working hard to break new ground, to find new directions for the theatre to better serve the region. The payoff is everywhere: in the quality of the performances you will see today, in the All-America City award the ASF helped bring to Anniston, in the wide recognition and acclaim we have received, and in the beginnings of a representative state Board. We look at these achievements with great pride. There is so much more to do.

Josephine E. Ayers, Chairman of the Board from 1976 to 1982 and Executive Producer from 1978 to 1982.

William J. Davis, Chairman of the ASF Board of Directors, 1974–75.

The ASF grew slowly but steadily within this part-time leadership structure, with the first year's expenses rounding out to $8,000; 1973 expenses climbing to $23,890; 1974 expenses rising to $32,140; and 1975 expenses hitting $50,466. During this period the Board of Directors kept a close watch on the overall balance sheet, and expenses and income were well controlled.

Early efforts to expand the base of support for the Festival included a push for educational tie-ins. An "ASF Workshop" was set up in the Anniston High School by a Board member in 1974. Birmingham was quickly targeted by the Board as an important source of funding and audience members, and the Board used personal contacts to bring the ASF to this neighboring city. An industrial sales program offering tickets at reduced rates to major corporations was introduced by Board President Davis. Also, Jacksonville State University was called on for company housing and educational support. The Board realized at this time that the Festival was going to have to reach out to a large segment of Alabama if the ASF planned to survive and grow.

Although Platt was always eager to label the ASF as a professional theatre, he and other staff members had great difficulty in the early years convincing the community and region that their organization wasn't just another community-based organization with only community appeal. Board President Davis addressed this issue in a letter to patrons on July 19, 1974:

> The activities of the Festival Board began last September with the selection of a new Board, the repertoire, and the development of a professional image. . . . the Alabama Shakespeare Festival is the only Shakespeare festival in the entire Southeast, and our performers are professional actors and actresses from different parts of the country.

Josephine E. Ayers echoed Davis's sentiments in a patron letter when she wrote:

> This is not an Anniston Festival. It belongs to all the people of Alabama through its designation as the official State Theatre, and therefore, the Board knows no geographical boundaries.

When Platt looks back on key moments of the Festival's history, he is quick to point to what he calls the "Bill Davis era" and the "Josephine Ayers regime." "When Bill Davis was President of the Board, we took some big but cautious leaps in the budget," explains Platt. At that time the Board President also functioned as a general business manager; Davis kept a tight rein on budgets, signed checks personally, and set up clear financial controls. As President of a local industry, Davis also assisted the ASF by donating materials and many trucking and printing services. According to Platt, "This made a major difference in the professional development of the ASF both on stage and in our public relations materials."

Many of the Festival's past Board members and staff also identify and categorize the character of the Board in relation to its two longest serving Board leaders: William J. Davis and Josephine E. Ayers. Davis was Board President from 1974 to 1975 and Board Chairman from 1976 to 1978, while Ayers took over as Board President in 1976 and led the Board through 1982. "Bill Davis and Josephine Ayers *ran* the Board," emphasized Platt. "They made decisions and moved ahead and most everyone else went along." As President, Board Chairman, and Executive Producer, Josephine E. Ayers offered leadership, vision, vibrance, and vitality to the ASF for over a decade. She captured the hearts of Shakespeare lovers throughout the Southeast, received formal tributes from the State Legislature, and was awarded the Governor's Arts Award for her work with the ASF.

A study of the ASF's historical records and personal conversations with Bill Davis and Josephine Ayers reveal the strong leadership qualities that helped the Festival grow and prosper. Their historical commitment to the community, to the stage, and to the artistic quality of the Alabama Shakespeare Festival helped pave the way to the ASF's current success.

In 1976, ASF expenses jumped to $77,550, and in 1977 they nearly doubled, ending up at $133,298. Virtually everyone on the ASF Board seemed to recognize the need for paid professional staff assistance as the ever-increasing budget raised the need for additional financial controls, fund-raising, marketing, and financial reporting. Unfortunately, plans to hire support staff were too often dependent upon the ASF's perceived ability to "afford" management staff. In a December 1975 report to the Board, Ayers explains that the Board's search for a large grant and a General Manager "depends entirely on our success in fund-raising." Six months later, Davis would write, "We need someone to coordinate all the activities of the Board on a regular basis, recognizing that there are very few people in the community who have the time or wherewithall to assume this responsibility. I don't know how we can afford to increase our expenses by a full-time Executive Director. The Festival, in my opinion, does not have the money."

The lack of any full-time management staff during this crucial period of major budget growth culminated in a myriad of administrative problems. From Platt's perspective, "It was okay to jump into the abyss and have a deficit, but we couldn't identify the major financial burdens or raise funds enough to cover the problems. Strong leadership on the Board helped fill a lack of management staff, helped in in-kind services and some fund-raising, but it really made it impossible to develop any real base of support within the whole Board. Instead of there being twenty people to deal with problems and development, there was only one."

In 1977, after six years without a professional theatre manager, the Alabama Shakespeare Festival Board of Directors finally gave the approval to launch a search, and Anne Zimmerman was hired to develop a long-range plan for the Festival, explore new ways to reach out and involve the surrounding communities, develop the educational resources of the Festival, and generate additional support and audiences for the expanding Festival. Having worked as the Assistant Business Manager for the North Shore Music Theatre in Massachusetts and the American Theatre Association in Washington, D.C., Zimmerman brought a knowledge of the arts and arts management to the Festival. With the support of the Foundation for the Extension and Development of the American Professional Theatre (FEDAPT), Zimmerman led the Festival to a 64 percent increase in earned income while attendance jumped 52 percent from 10,063 in 1976 to over 15,000 in 1977. Although contributions increased, they still fell short of the Board's budget, and the ASF was forced to scramble to avert a major deficit. Again in 1978, attendance increased dramatically to 23,000, but the expenses also rose significantly; both the earned and unearned portions of the budget fell short of the Board's projections.

Still, the deficits remained controllable, and although expenses had more than tripled from $77,550 in 1976 to $252,376 in 1978, Zimmerman was able to keep the Festival financially stable by maximizing box office income and subsidiary income such as program advertising and concessions. In her first season with the Festival, Zimmerman wrote:

> I am extremely fortunate to have the support and guidance of the Festival's Board of Directors. It is because of their breadth of vision and dedication that the Festival has grown into a project of regional significance. As the only theatre of its kind between Washington and Dallas, the Festival is in a unique position to provide the Southeast with great entertainment, cultural enrichment, and educational opportunities. The possibilities are almost limitless.

Although the commitment from the Board was no doubt in place, the reality of the situation was that unearned income would not be able to keep pace with the rise in earned income and overall expenses.

The regional theatre boom and development of major regional and national subsidies for the arts in the early 1970s went largely unnoticed in the southeastern United States. Most Southern cities pulled together community sponsored and funded chorale groups and other music groups, and a number of community theatres were spawned in cities

Anne F. Zimmerman, ASF Managing Director from 1977 to 1979.

throughout the South. However, regional theatres with professional aspirations and national importance remained a phenomenon of the North, East, and West with little support or understanding of such operations in the South. Anniston and the surrounding communities were no exception. Without a history of major theatrical support, either through attendance or contributions, the Alabama Shakespeare Festival had to break new ground and pioneer a fresh look at theatre production and support in the Southeast.

The ASF Board of Directors and staff found themselves in the position of continually working to educate and train their patrons, area businesses, regional corporations, state legislators, and national arts supporters. They bombarded these patrons and potential patrons with pleas and statistics regarding contributed income. Various national arts supporters, including the National Endowment for the Arts and other foundations, were approached in an effort to educate and convince them of the artistic growth and potential of professional theatre in the South. The ongoing message was simple—professional theatre is good business economically, culturally, socially, and educationally.

These lobbying efforts and educational processes have been continuing activities for over a dozen years for the Alabama Shakespeare Festival staff and Board of Directors. It has become increasingly clear throughout the 1970s and 1980s that professional theatre cannot survive in the United States without support from outside the box office. As discussed previously, the early years of the Alabama Shakespeare Festival were financially simple ones. Expense budgets were frugal, income projections were cautious, and the overall finances were clearly controlled. These were fiscally happy and fairly predictable financial years for the Festival as few of the major professional theatre budgeting hazards had yet descended upon the ASF. Cash flow, or "working capital" concerns were seldom a significant problem as pre-season ticket sales and contributions virtually covered the nominal start-up costs and salaries for seasonal employees. Since there weren't any year-round employees, fulfilling off-season payroll requirements and covering overhead expenses weren't necessary.

The Alabama Shakespeare Festival had remained a nonunion theatre. As a result, there weren't any of the uncontrollable wage increases, personnel demands, company size requirements, and benefit packages that would later threaten the financial stability of many of America's arts operations, including the Alabama Shakespeare Festival. Festival officials maintained total control over all salaries and production costs and made reasonable income projections during the budgeting period.

It is likely, and perhaps fortunate, that neither Platt nor the ASF Board of Directors were aware of the tremendous odds against a successful major theatre operation in Anniston when they began their

Martin L. Platt's updated version of Macbeth *features Bruce Cromer as MacDuff and Jack Wetherall as MacBeth, 1984.*

efforts. Since there wasn't anyone around the Alabama arts community who could forewarn the ASF staff and Board that their proposed annual project was an impossible dream, they had free rein to succeed in the face of almost absolute adversity. Although little research and few finely honed professional theatre skills were involved in the beginnings of Festival, those individuals who committed their time and efforts to the project brought about its many successes, artistically and financially, throughout the early and mid-1970s. It wasn't until the budget grew into six figures that controlling costs, estimating income, and overall financial planning became crucial issues regarding the ongoing survival of the Alabama Shakespeare Festival.

Major financial problems didn't surface until after the year-round staff additions were instituted during 1977 and 1978. The commitment to full-time staff salaries, an expanded season, additional Equity actors, and the subsequent increased marketing needs were a logical outgrowth of the financial expectations and artistic aspirations of the Artistic Director and Board of Directors. The expansion was also the partial result of a consultancy organized by the Foundation for the Extension and Development of the American Professional Theatre (FEDAPT). In a meeting with the ASF Board of Directors and staff, Frederic Vogel, Executive Director of FEDAPT, explained his feelings about the ASF:

> The Alabama Shakespeare Festival is truly an impressive story, not because of the article in *The New York Times,* and not because it is the South and Alabama. What is impressive to me is that with as few number of people in this area that you have managed not only to survive but to grow to the extent you have grown. If you make a comparison with the rest of the country, you compare quite favorably. It takes five to ten years to set up such an operation and you are pretty solid for only five years. Thank you for enhancing the theatre of this country. You have done an incredible job.

The first season after Vogel's visit (the 1977 season), the ASF increased its Actor's Equity company from one to fourteen, massively increased marketing efforts, significantly increased production budgets, and increased its total expenses over 85 percent from $77,550 in 1976 to $133,298 in 1977. In the five-year period from 1977 through 1981, the Alabama Shakespeare Festival's company grew to include nearly twenty Equity actors, and a major tour of the Southeast was added in the fall after the summer repertory season. On the financial side, actual expenses grew by over 1,000 percent from $77,550 in 1976 to $785,887 in 1982.

In budgeting an operation as complicated as a five-play professional repertory theatre, planners must take a number of factors into account: the frequency of productions, the length of the performance run, the number of performances, the climate, the geographical location, the physical plant conditions, the seating capacity, the number of theatres in operation, and the general overhead and maintenance needs of the operation. It is difficult to ascertain whether or not the Alabama Shakespeare Festival Board of Directors and administrative staff were projecting reasonable expectations in annual income levels or whether the Festival's fund-raising was simply not strong enough or sufficiently executed to achieve the budgeted goals. Either way, the end-of-year results planted the seeds of disenchantment that would grow into serious financial problems for the Alabama Shakespeare Festival and less than satisfied encounters between the Alabama Shakespeare Festival Board of Directors and key executive staff in the late 1970s and early 1980s.

In an article on establishing good relations with Boards of Directors, William Stewart, Managing Director of the Hartford Stage Company, writes:

> Management must provide the Board with timely, consistent, concise, and accurate information. Boards of Trustees/Directors cannot be expected to make reasonable and appropriate decisions on broad policy without direction and guidance from a sensitive and clear management . . . a good Managing Director should not surprise the Board, and more importantly, never surprise the President . . . too often, divisiveness results when Board members do not meet their accepted fundraising objectives or when management falls short of its earned income projections.

Michael Maso, ASF's Managing Director from 1980 to 1982.

Michael Maso, an arts management consultant for the New Mexico Arts Commission and former Business Manager for the PAF Playhouse in Long Island, replaced Zimmerman in 1980 and took over the administration of the Festival. According to Martin L. Platt:

> Anne Zimmerman's contributions to the ASF were marketing and selling tickets. She was a workaholic and was dedicated to the Festival because she believed in it and wanted to make it work. Michael Maso's strengths were in dealing with people—forming strong bonds of loyalty with staff and Board members. He's a good negotiator and was easy to work with because he was interested in the artistic product and in making the artistic product work.

Although the Festival's artistic offerings grew and improved significantly during the early 1980s, the Board wasn't prepared for the major deficits that accompanied the larger operations. By December 1981, the ASF deficit had grown in excess of $180,000, and an accountant consulting for the Board set the cash liabilities of the Alabama Shakespeare Festival in March 1982 at closer to $279,000.

"So foul and fair a day I have not seen."

MACBETH

The ASF "Second Decade" campaign helped trim the deficit, but with over $160,000 in remaining liabilities and the threat of the 1982 season's cancellation, the Alabama Shakespeare Festival Executive Committee negotiated a contract with Mr. Winton M. Blount that would secure the future of the Festival and eventually allow Platt to fulfill his dream of producing year-round in a new theatre home specifically created for the Alabama Shakespeare Festival and classical repertory theatre.

The 1983 and 1984 seasons in Anniston were two of the brightest seasons in the Festival's history. Both seasons were deemed artistically magnificent and this period of time will always be remembered as the beginning of the ASF's remarkable financial turnaround. The Anniston Board members who were instrumental in these record-breaking seasons included Josephine E. Ayers, Ann M. Barker, John Childs, Inga Davis, William J. Davis, Juliette Doster, Farley Galbraith, Richard Hensley, Charles E. Johnson, John Kelly, Austin Letson, Thomas Malone, E. Guice Potter, Jr., Thomas Stinson, William Talbot, Jr., Abby Ulrey, Jean Willett, and Alice Donald.

As part of the overall expansion, transition, and long-range planning process in late 1982, various members of the ASF Board of Directors pressed for new administrative leadership. Jim Volz was appointed Managing Director and John E. Kelly was elected as the new Chairman of the Board of Directors. According to Platt:

> The immediate quality that Jim Volz brought to ASF was steadiness and firmness in management. Jim quickly took control of the Board and staff and imposed strict financial and budget controls. Although each new day seemed to unearth new financial nightmares, Jim managed to survive the onslaught and pull ASF, truly singlehandedly, from deep red ink and questionable business practices to black ink and a clean slate.

Volz attributed the record-breaking ticket sales, fund-raising efforts, nationally acclaimed artistic product, creation of the new Professional Actor Training/Master of Fine Arts Program, organization of the Consortium for Academic Programs, and overall institutionalization of the ASF in the mid-1980s to the joint efforts of a hard working artistic, administrative, and production staff and an unselfish, dedicated, and inspired Board of Directors. He especially noted the efforts of Board Chairman John Kelly and executive committee member Juliette Doster, who were pivotal players in the ASF's overall operation and leaders in the record-breaking fund-raising campaigns in 1983 and 1984. According to Volz, "Juliette Doster and John Kelly's personal support and tireless efforts on behalf of the ASF helped us to reach our full potential as dedicated citizens and as a national arts force of the highest caliber."

John Kelly, Chairman of the ASF Board of Directors, 1983–85.

In representing the Board of Directors, John E. Kelly provided warmth, directness, history of business clout and support of the ASF that set the example for other Board members and all of the ASF's supporters. In a public tribute to Chairman Kelly in 1985, the Board of Directors voiced their appreciation:

> We instinctively turned to John Kelly for direction and for vision. He responded, as he always has, by saying, "Yes, this needs me and deserves my help." John Kelly, son of a labor organizer, a Yankee from Connecticut, operator of a mill supply and hardware house, who still speaks in a Yankee-Irish brogue, would ostensibly seem the antithesis of a Shakespeare fan, much less a desirable contender for the throne of the Shakespeare Festival, especially in Alabama. The past two seasons of leadership under John Kelly were two of the most exciting the ASF has ever known. In two short years, John Kelly pioneered new artistic programs, increases in City funding, a massive growth in overall contributed income, and an exciting partnership with the Committee for the Humanities, which resulted in a $75,000 grant from the National Endowment for the Humanities and the statewide program "Shakespeare: Theatre in the Mind." It is impossible to consider the fate of the Alabama Shakespeare Festival had not John Kelly assumed the Presidency in 1983.

The story of the Alabama Shakespeare Festival Board of Directors is a miraculous one in many ways. The Board of Directors and its many support groups (including the ASF Volunteer Guild of 200 dedicated women and the ASF Junior Guild of enthusiastic young women), were instrumental in the ASF's growth from a tiny community-spawned theatrical troupe into a major regional theatre. The Board of Directors historically worked without financial compensation, little thanks, and sparse recognition for a cause that they believed in. At a time when few citizens realized the social, cultural, economic, and educational worth of the Festival, many key Board members worked year after year to sustain the ASF in Anniston.

The Anniston Board was a very trusting, giving, supportive, and involved group. Their personal commitment is evident in the financial and artistic records of the Festival throughout its history—financial contributions, in-kind contributions, property donations, fund-raising, space and property loans, time commitments, and personal lobbying on the city, county, state, and federal levels. Platt's dream of a professional theatre was fleshed out by those volunteers who pulled the entire operation together from 1972 through the present day.

The strength of the Board of Directors continues through the 1980s as an enlarged Board of representatives from throughout the State of Alabama and region oversees the current operation and plans for the future. In 1985, a prestigious group of Montgomery leaders was added to the Board roster, including the Mayor of Montgomery, Emory Folmar. According to past Chairman and longtime Board member William J. Davis, "The initial support of key people in the Montgomery community is evidence of Montgomery's commitment to this outstanding project which will be a landmark for the nation."

Joining the Board as new members in 1985 were Winton M. Blount, Chairman of the Board and Chief Executive Officer of Blount, Inc.; Reverend G. Murray Branch, Pastor, Dexter Avenue King Memorial Baptist Church; Charles Brightwell, General Manager, Montgomery Coca-Cola Bottling Company; Margaret Carpenter, President of Composit; Fran Cleveland, Director of Arts Activities, Fitzpatrick Associates; Taylor Dawson, President, Andrew & Dawson, Inc.; Tranum Fitzpatrick, President, Governors House Associates; Mayor Emory Folmar, The City of Montgomery; Doyle Harvill, Publisher, The Advertiser Company; Elmore Inscoe; Knox Kershaw, President, Knox Kershaw, Inc.; Henry Leslie, President and Chief Executive Officer, Union Bank and Trust company; Joan Loeb; Peggy Mussafer, Interior Consultant, Peggy Mussafer Interiors; Dr. Guin A. Nance, Vice-Chancellor for Academic Affairs, Auburn University at Montgomery; Judge Charles Price, Montgomery County Circuit Judge; Lt. General Thomas C. Richards, Commander of Air University, Maxwell Air Force Base; James Scott, Attorney, Cappell, Howard, Knabe, and Cobbs; Philip A. Sellers, President, Philip A. Sellers & Co., Inc.; John M. Trotman, Owner, Trotman Land and Cattle Company; Charles Whitehurst, General Manager and Vice-President, WSFA-TV; Jim Wilson, Jr., President, Jim Wilson and Associates, Inc.

Anniston Board members continuing their terms on the Board were Ann M. Barker, English Department Head, Donoho School; Carolyn Blount; Joanna Bosko, Cultural Arts Supervisor, Parks and Recreation Department, The City of Montgomery; John Childs, Assistant to the President, *Anniston Star;* Inga L. Davis, Past President, the Alabama Shakespeare Festival Guild; William J. Davis, Past President of the Alabama Shakespeare Festival Board of Directors; Juliette Doster, Past President, the Alabama Shakespeare Festival Guild; Kate Durr Elmore, Instructor, Auburn University; Jan Howard; Wilbur Hufham, President and Chief Executive Officer, First Alabama Bank of Montgomery; John Kelly, Retired Owner, Kelly Supply; Austin Letson, Chairman of Regional Health Services, Inc., and President of North East Alabama Regional Medical Center; E. Guice Potter, Jr., City Chairman of the Board, AmSouth Bank, N.A.; Abby Ulrey, Past Vice-President and Charter Member, the Alabama Shakespeare Festival Guild; and Jean Willett, Past President, the Alabama Shakespeare Festival Guild.

After a solid base of support was established in Montgomery, there was a major push to add regional board members. The following were added: Jane S. Comer, Birmingham; Emory Cunningham, Chief Executive Officer, Southern Progress Corporation, Birmingham; Suzanne G. Elson, Atlanta; Sarah Hardaway, Midland, Georgia; Emil Hess, Chairman of the Board, Parisian, Inc., Birmingham; J. L. Lanier, Chairman of the Board, West Point-Pepperell, Inc., West Point, Georgia; Wallace D. Malone, Jr., Chairman of the Board and CEO, SouthTrust Bank Corporation, Birmingham; Perry Mendel, Chairman of the Board, Kindercare Learning Centers, Inc., Montgomery; Sara Moore, Atlanta; Danne B. Munford, Atlanta; G. Harold Northrop, President and CEO, Callaway Gardens, Pine Mountain, Georgia; Dr. Benjamin F. Payton, President, Tuskegee University, Tuskegee, Alabama; Jane Weinberger, Washington, D.C.; and John W. Woods, Chairman of the Board and CEO, AmSouth Bank.

Philip A. Sellers, Chairman of the Alabama Shakespeare Festival Board of Directors, 1985 to present.

One of the first acts of the expanded Board was to appoint Philip A. Sellers, one of Alabama's most prominent citizens, Chairman of the statewide Board of Directors. A graduate of Washington and Lee University, Philip A. Sellers was a natural choice to lead the Board through this exciting expansion period. His dedication to the Montgomery area included service as a past president of the Rotary Club, United Way, and the Montgomery Council on the Aging. As Chairman of the Board of Trustees of Huntingdon College and past president of the Montgomery Chamber of Commerce, Sellers offered the ASF the warmth, leadership, and strength necessary to build a world-class theatre.

This Board of Directors paved the way for many of the ASF's most successful theatrical productions and artistic programs. Their work in the community and throughout the state helped encourage the support and enthusiasm of audience members, arts administrators, the university community, and many other resources that are of the utmost importance to the ASF.

Robert H. Craft, Jr., who serves as a trustee of the Washington Opera, once asserted:

> The ways in which a working board can contribute to the strength of the organization are limited only by the imagination of its leadership and dedication of its members.

The Alabama Shakespeare Festival Board of Directors, along with the artistic company, has comprised the backbone of the ASF and is the major reason the Festival has emerged as one of America's finest professional theatres.

Historical Listing of ASF Board of Directors

"Upon your sword sit laurel victory! And smooth success be strew'd before your feet!"

ANTONY AND CLEOPATRA

CHAIRMEN

Philip A. Sellers, 1985–
John Kelly, 1983–1985
Josephine E. Ayers, 1976–1982

William J. Davis, 1974–1975
B. C. Moore, 1973

MEMBERS OF THE BOARD

William P. Acker, III
H. Brandt Ayers
Josephine E. Ayers
Ann M. Barker
Jean Berry
Carolyn S. Blount
Winton M. Blount
Joanna Bosko
Rev. G. Murray Branch
Charles Brightwell
Olive Burt
Richard Byrd
Ralph W. Callahan
James Campbell
Margaret Carpenter
John Childs
Michael H. Cleckler
Fran Cleveland
Jane S. Comer
Emory Cunningham
Inga L. Davis
William J. Davis
Taylor Dawson
George Deyo
Alice Donald
Juliette P. Doster
James A. Dunn
Kate Durr Elmore
Suzanne G. Elson
William M. Falkenberry
Arthur Fite, III
Tranum Fitzpatrick
Emory Folmar

Hank Freeman
John Fulmer
Farley M. Galbraith
William Gauntt
Glenn Gordon
Margaret Griffis
Sarah Hardaway
Doyle Harvill
Richard Hensley
Emil Hess
Jan Howard
Hoyt W. Howell
Wilbur Hufham
Elmore Inscoe
Julian W. Jenkins
Charles E. Johnson
Tora Johnson
John Kelly
Knox Kershaw
Joseph Kingston
J. L. Lanier
Henry Leslie
Austin Letson
Lynn Letson
Joan Loeb
E. Thomas Malone
Wallace D. Malone
Perry Mendel
George A. Monk
Theron Montgomery
Gloria Moody
B. C. Moore
Sara Moore

Danné B. Munford
Peggy Mussafer
Guin A. Nance
G. Harold Northrop
George O. Parker
Benjamin F. Payton
Thomas Peterson
E. Guice Potter, Jr.
Beatrice Potts
Thomas Potts
Charles Price
Thomas Quinn
Thomas C. Richards
Margaret Rilling
Anne Roberts
Eugene Rutledge
James Scott
Philip A. Sellers
Daisy Weller Smith
Rita G. Springer
Thomas Stinson
Jill Stockton
William Talbot, Jr.
John M. Trotman
Betty W. Tyler
Abby Ulrey
Jane Weinberger
Charles Whitehurst
Jean Willett
Jim Wilson, Jr.
John W. Woods

Margaret Griffis, ASF Guild President from 1977 to 1978.

Inga Davis, President of the ASF Guild from 1974 to 1975.

Alice Donald, ASF Guild President from 1982 to 1984.

Left: Juliette Doster, ASF Guild President from 1975 to 1977.

Right: Tora Johnson, ASF Guild President in 1984 and from 1978 to 1980.

From left to right: Betty Potts, Founder and President of the ASF Guild in 1973 and 1974; and Jean Willett, Guild President from 1980 to 1982.

Ex officio

ASF EXECUTIVE STAFF

Martin L. Platt
Artistic Director, 1972–Present

Jim Volz
Managing Director, 1982–Present

Josephine E. Ayers
Executive Producer, 1978–1982

Michael Maso
Managing Director, 1980–1982

Anne F. Zimmerman
Managing Director, 1977–1979

The beautiful new ASF complex designed by Blount/Pittman and Associates and contributed as a gift to the State of Alabama and the nation by Winton M. and Carolyn Blount.

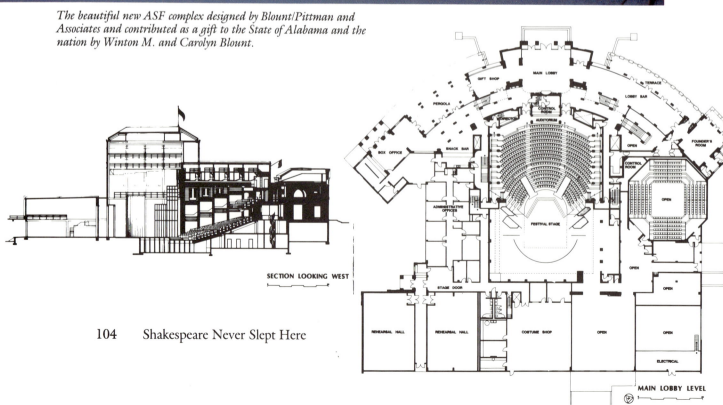

SECTION LOOKING WEST

104   Shakespeare Never Slept Here

MAIN LOBBY LEVEL

IV

A Look to the Future

America's theatre movement outside of New York has been a source of intense controversy and study for the past twenty years. Many professionals insist that the nationwide theatre movement outside of New York *is* the American Theatre and scoff at the term "regional theatre" which they see as the movement's insecure attempt to define itself in relation to New York City.

Whatever label one may attach to the rising number of theatres cropping up in cities throughout the nation, it is clear that no label can begin to identify the artistic dreams and objectives or management structures and histories that are personal to each organization. However, despite the various institutional differences, goals, processes, and styles, there are still many common threads that bind America's theatres together. Edward A. Martenson, Director of the National Endowment for the Arts' Theatre Program, offers some background on the history of the movement:

Cathleen Owens in the new ASF administrative offices in Montgomery.

> The nonprofit resident theatre movement is scarcely more than twenty years old. It was begun in a state of high idealism by talented artists who wanted to work with a continuity and seriousness of purpose not possible in commercial theatre. The impulse which gave birth to the movement was profoundly artistic in nature—not financial, not geographical—but artistic. These high artistic ideals have guided the theatres, even though practical details of day-to-day management increasingly have created a gap between the ideals and the achievement.

Over 25,000 students join in the exciting ASF SchoolFest program, which offers professional theatre throughout the school year.

"The best is yet to do."

AS YOU LIKE IT

Simon Bovinett and Carol Ogus in the Montgomery administrative offices.

Although the impulse that pulled many of the nation's theatres together may have been based on artistic genius, the reality that is ripping many of the theatres apart centers on management. Virtually every area of nonprofit theatre management is a crucial part of each and every regional theatre operation: marketing, development, Board of Directors partnerships, public relations, volunteerism, personnel management, and staffing.

The ASF Partnership

Fortunately, the partnership created in the mid-1980s between educators, legislators, Board members, and businessmen throughout Alabama helped the Alabama Shakespeare Festival to grow and prosper. The remarkable rally of statewide support thrust the city of Montgomery and the state of Alabama into the nation's theatrical spotlight, and the attention was well deserved. The unique partnership between private citizens, city officials, the State Legislature, the Governor, university leaders, corporate sponsors, the State Arts Council, and the Alabama Shakespeare Festival emerged as a model for the nation. The results were staggering. During the short expansion period in 1984 and 1985:

1) *State support for the ASF increased from $30,000 to $750,000.* Governor George C. Wallace and the Alabama Legislature stunned the nation with this major appropriation, and their vision and support for the State Theatre and its far-reaching cultural and educational goals were solidly backed by Chamber of Commerce statistics that project the ASF's economic impact at over $90 million. This monumental contribution in important areas of the state's economy and artistic and educational heritage includes projections of over $800,000 in city, county, and state sales tax and $1.25 million in personal income.

2) *City of Montgomery funding jumped to over $300,000.* Montgomery Mayor Emory Folmar and Council members Herchel Christian, Billy Turner, Joe Reed, Mark Gilmore, Jr., Joseph Dickerson, Leu Hammonds, Alice Reynolds, Bud Chambers, and William Nunn hailed the Theatre as "a fine new industry" and assisted the ASF during the transition and opening in a myriad of ways.

3) *Montgomery businessmen pledged their support in efforts to raise an additional $300,000 in community funding.* Swept into the wave of enthusiasm generated by the city and state's support, the leadership of Montgomery's Business Committee for the Arts promoted major fund-raising campaigns that helped create a local awareness of the ASF's financial needs and artistic goals.

It's a glorious day for the Bard. . . .
I've seen all the great Shakespearean
houses on earth, and there is none that
compares to this!

Actor Tony Randall
December 7, 1985

Guest celebrity Tony Randall shares the stage with special guest Olivia de Havilland to welcome the Gala crowd and pay tribute to the many people who support the Alabama Shakespeare Festival.

You cannot imagine the joy and privilege and honor it is for me to be here participating in the dedication of this beautiful, beautiful theatre. It must be unique in all the world—I hope to return time and time again. What a gift it is to Montgomery, Alabama, the Southeast, and to the nation. You've heard the saying, 'The South Will Rise Again' . . . with this theatre you have started it on its way!

Actress Olivia de Havilland

The front lobby leading to the patron's room in the new ASF Complex in Montgomery.

4) *Regional corporate leaders contributed hundreds of thousands of dollars through sponsorships of special programs.* In efforts to support the State Theatre, corporate businessmen offered substantial amounts of money to support the ASF's educational programs and specific plays.

5) *University leaders throughout Alabama joined hands to support the ASF by creating the Consortium for Academic Programs.* In an effort to increase the base of support and impact of the Alabama Shakespeare Festival throughout the state of Alabama, key members of each of the state's nineteen senior state educational institutions were asked to attend a planning session at Auburn University in Auburn, Alabama. In a remarkable show of support and enthusiasm, the universities and colleges joined together to promote the mutual interests of the ASF and the state's academic community. In a statement of purpose ratified by thirty-eight institutional representatives, the Consortium for Academic Programs clarified its major objectives:

The Consortium for Academic Programs serves as a coordinating agency between its member institutions and the Alabama Shakespeare Festival for the purpose of providing support and advice to the Alabama Shakespeare Festival from the academic institutions of Alabama and to allow for the involvement of the institutions in the work of the Festival in whatever ways are appropriate. The members of the Consortium believe that the Shakespeare Festival is one of the great human resources of the State of Alabama and formed themselves into this Consortium in the belief that significant benefits will accrue to both the Festival and to the academic community from this interchange.

The Consortium has already assisted the ASF in lobbying for state funding, marketing the new complex, setting up internships and educational opportunities for students, and creating new training and cultural programs for the Festival and for the state of Alabama.

6) *The University of Alabama and the ASF entered into agreements to create the state's first Professional Actor Training/Master of Fine Arts Program (PAT/MFA).* As part of the Consortium's efforts, Dr. Edward C. Moore, Senior Vice Chancellor of the University of Alabama system led

Titania and the Fairies in A Midsummer Night's Dream, *1985.*

delicate negotiations between university officials and the ASF Executive Staff. An exciting two-year graduate program resulted and provides the opportunity for fifteen talented actors to study, train, and perform full time in the ASF complex. The faculty of the program is headed by James Donadio and includes members of the professional acting company and experienced educators from throughout the nation.

7) *The Alabama State Arts Council approved a total of $80,000 for student and community support of ASF student matinee programs and a major professional tour of* The Glass Menagerie. This partnership project called for substantial joint funding for the innovative SchoolFest student matinee program, which allows Alabama students to purchase $15 ASF theatre tickets for only $4. The project also assists even the smallest Alabama communities in their efforts to book major ASF touring productions. Spearheaded by ASF Educational Services Director Carol Ogus and General Manager Doug Perry, this project came to fruition in large part due to the vision of new Alabama Arts Council Director Al Head and the members of the ASCAH grants review committee.

According to State Superintendent of Education, Dr. Wayne Teague:

> The Shakespeare Festival will greatly enhance the cultural offerings both for Montgomerians and all Alabamians statewide. The Shakespeare Festival will be of particular significance to the school children of the State. . . . I believe the Shakespeare Festival will aid in the development of higher order intellectual skills, and I would encourage every student to participate to the fullest extent possible.

8) *The Committee for the Humanities in Alabama and the National Endowment for the Humanities in Washington, D.C., approved over $70,000 in funding for a nationally acclaimed humanities project "Shakespeare: Theatre in the Mind."* The project provides educational tabloids and study guides that focus on ASF productions, while the far-reaching educational sessions have included visits by internationally known theatre professionals Jonathan Miller and O. B. Hardison. The statewide participatory project was the brainstorm of Humanities' staff members Walter Cox, Christine Reilly, Mary Hix, and members of the ASF Staff.

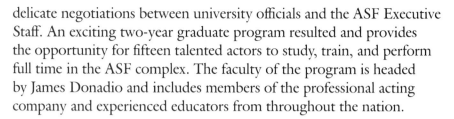

Robert Browning as Tom in the 1985–86 ASF production of The Glass Menagerie.

Below: Evelyn Carol Case as Hermia and Bruce Cromer as Lysander in the 1985–86 ASF comedy, A Midsummer Night's Dream.

"The poet that holds up to his reader a faithful mirror of manners and of life"—thus affording us "the stability of truth." (Samuel Johnson Preface to *Shakespeare's Works*, 1765) Quality of life is very important to the overall good of our community. I firmly believe the presence of the Alabama Shakespeare Festival will enhance the quality of life in Montgomery. The citizens of Montgomery will be forever grateful to the Blount family for making the Alabama Shakespeare Festival at Wynfield a reality.

Emory Folmar, *Mayor*
City of Montgomery

Left: A "rustics toast" in the 1985–86 ASF production of A Midsummer Night's Dream.

Below: Cast members of A Midsummer Night's Dream *at ASF in 1985–86.*

Bottom: Robert Browning and Joan Ulmer in the premiere show, The Glass Menagerie, *show in the ASF's new 225-seat theatre, the Octagon. (1985)*

The ASF's New Home

As one might suspect, the spark for this statewide outpouring of assistance was former Postmaster General Winton M. "Red" and Carolyn Blount's magnificent $21.5 million contribution of a new fully equipped two-theatre home in the state capital. This new facility allows the ASF to expand into year-round operations featuring over a dozen major plays, musical concerts, educational programs, and an array of other events.

Red Blount's corporate collection of fine art, support of many art forms, and overall commitment to the arts in Alabama is legendary. His interest is genuine and informed:

> It may be difficult to define the exact role of the arts in our community life, although we are increasingly aware of their importance. Obviously the arts have much to do with the quality of life. . . . The presence of cultural activities is a potent force in helping to make a city attractive to the new breed of college graduates and younger people who have a strong social and cultural awareness.
>
> So it is a matter of enlightened self-interest for business to support the arts. And it is a matter of good corporate citizenship. But most of all, it is a matter of making our community a better place to live for those of us who take great pride in calling it home.

"We are building a theatre second to none to provide the finest Shakespeare in this land and beyond," explained Winton M. Blount in 1985. And indeed, the 97,000-square-foot complex is a contemporary marvel of theatrical technology. In addition to the 750-seat Festival

Olivia de Havilland, Winton M. Blount, and Carolyn Blount arrive for the ASF's Gala opening of A Midsummer Night's Dream.

The lobby and stairs leading to the Octagon in the new ASF complex designed by Blount/Pittman and Associates.

Celebrity guests Marion Ross (Happy Days), *Michael Learned, and Mary McDonough* (The Waltons), *and film star John Schuck join the ASF for the premiere performances in December 1985.*

ASF staff and members of the national press gather in the ASF patron's room, designed by Glenn Bear and Ford McGowin of Bear-McGowin Interiors.

This theatre has been a work of love for Carolyn and me. I have been inspired by her interest and knowledge of Shakespeare and this has guided me in my developing appreciation. It is a privilege for both of us to give this theatre to the people of the United States and to the generations of the future. It will stand as an enduring tribute of love to my wife, Carolyn, and it is my desire that it be known forever as The Carolyn Blount Theatre.

Winton M. Blount
Dedicated December 1985

Longtime Board member E. Guice Potter and his wife, Pat, arrive for the Gala opening.

ASF actor Charles Antalosky and television celebrity Polly Holliday enjoy cocktails in the ASF lobby.

Out-of-town guests Frances Coonrod and Lou Case join the Gala festivities.

Pat Doty, designer Michael Stauffer, and Jim Greco prepare for the opening of the Festival Stage.

Al Hirt entertains the Gala night crowd following the spectacular opening of A Midsummer Night's Dream *on December 7, 1985.*

A Look to the Future   113

A curtain call on the Festival Stage for the 1985-86 A Midsummer Night's Dream.

Stage and the 225-seat theatre, the Octagon, the complex houses administrative offices, two rehearsal halls, costume, scenery, and properties shops, a gift shop, cafe, and box office.

Blount/Pittman and Associated Architects, P.C., devised the master plan for the complex, designed on a "fast-track" with strong cooperation between the patrons, the contractor, and the Alabama Shakespeare Festival. The overall site is a 250-acre private estate labeled Wynfield Park. Included in the master plan of the estate is the ASF complex, an amphitheatre, an exact replica of Shakespeare's birthplace, a museum of fine arts, a house museum, and a concert hall. According to architect Thomas A. Blount, the extensive landscaping for the grounds was devised by Russell Page, hailed by the Royal Horticultural Society as "the most revered garden-maker of the mid-20th century." Before his death in January 1985, Russell Page worked closely with Blount/Pittman and Associated Architects, P.C., to develop the master plan, as well as the structure of the landscape surrounding the theatre.

"I have liv'd to see inherited my very wishes and the buildings of my fancy."

CORIOLANUS

Two New Theatres

Arrayed on eight levels, the 97,000 square feet of the major complex centers on the Festival Stage and the Octagon. The 750-seat Festival Stage is designed as a modified thrust adaptable for proscenium theatre use. The proscenium width is thirty-four feet. The stage of the Festival Stage is trapped in four-foot sections and there are eighty-three counterweighted linesets and five winched battens that operate from a grid-iron sixty-five feet above stage level. The stage is sixty-nine feet deep. The overall theatre is completely protected by sound and light locks that isolate the theatre from the rest of the complex.

Special efforts were made to keep the theatres extremely intimate and to provide for handicapped accessibility to all areas of the auditorium. An infrared sound enhancement system for the hearing impaired is an added attraction of the theatre.

Another unique feature of this twentieth-century theatre are six boxes that provide for side seating of special guests and contributors.

The smaller Octagon is a theatre designed for use as an arena, thrust, or proscenium theatre. The theatre seats 225 patrons and is used by the ASF for major productions, experimental shows, and graduate student training.

Public and Backstage Areas

The public areas of the ASF complex are designed for use of both theatregoers and other visitors to the area. A patron's room is available to contributors to the theatre and for special community and corporate events. The lobby areas relating to the Octagon and the Festival Stage have individual identities and are arranged to be used separately when both theatres are in operation. Support spaces include a large elevator, scenery storage, lighting storage, a coatroom, display space, a first aid room, modular bars, three control rooms, a director's room, and special spaces for video monitors.

Property, paint, scenery, costume, wig, and millinery shops combine with dressing rooms and design studios for production use. An actor's lounge and administrative offices for the marketing, development, educational, finance, box office, artistic, and executive staff round out the backstage areas.

Architecture and Interiors

The complex itself is made up of over one million brick units, which comprise the body of the building exterior and interior. The brick has been nicknamed "Shakespeare Blend" by the manufacturer and has become the manufacturer's best-selling brick!

The concrete roof decks feature lead-coated copper with coated copper roof accessories and are accentuated by green-tinted glass throughout the complex. The glass is framed in white oak window wall units in the public areas and in aluminum units in the backstage areas. Custom-designed and specially woven carpets lie on New York bluestone floors, and the floors in the patron's room are planks of nineteenth-century native heart pine. Furnishings in the public areas are designed to be sparse, consisting of custom modular benches that reflect the bronze and steel railings.

Thomas A. Blount and L. Perry Pittman joined in partnership to design the ASF complex. With offices in midtown Atlanta, Blount/Pittman and Associated Architects, P.C., brought a combined total of forty-five years professional experience to the project, ranging from historic preservation to speculative commercial buildings.

The varied backgrounds and complementary abilities of Thomas A. Blount and L. Perry Pittman have produced a team capable of approaching architectural problems with a unique perspective. The excellence in design and the commitment to close involvement of all concerned parties throughout the architectural process has resulted in one of the finest professional theatres in the world.

Building an Institution

The ASF has been fortunate in comparison to many regional theatres in that it has avoided the burden of raising "brick and mortar" money for the construction of the new complex. The remarkable gift of Carolyn and Winton M. "Red" Blount paid for all construction costs, considered by most theatre fund-raisers as the most difficult money to secure. The new facility enables the Festival to continue to improve the quality and accessibility of its productions, to branch out into increased educational services, and to host the world's leading performers and ensembles.

The Blounts' astounding contribution also served as a catalyst for state, regional, and national support from all areas. Aside from the above-mentioned city, state, and university support, major businesses and a unique array of nonprofit corporations suggested exciting new tie-ins to classical drama, Shakespeare, and the Alabama Shakespeare Festival. For example, the Coca-Cola Company proposed audience development support and the printing of over one million information items for potential ASF theatregoers; the major local newspaper, *The Montgomery Advertiser,* offered to print thousands of copies of the ASF history and 1985–1986 theatre schedules as a service to ASF patrons; and the Montgomery Museum of Fine Art created a dynamic Shakespeare exhibit featuring many of the world's finest Shakespeare art treasures.

National Attention and Sold-Out Houses

1985 was a year of happy surprises for Shakespeare in Alabama as the ASF garnered ongoing national attention and daily regional attention thanks to the many newspapers, radio, and television stations that created a grassroots awareness of the ASF's educational programs and the myriad of music, dance, and theatre performances. In the words of one exuberant board member, "Culture is gaining on agriculture for the first time in Alabama!"

Needless to say, part of the ASF Board of Directors' enthusiasm was the ASF staff's ability to build a solid financial base. Following three consecutive years of deficit spending in the early 1980s, the ASF staged a remarkable financial turnaround between 1983 and 1986 that included record setting in all income categories, and the creation of cash reserves and two separate endowment programs.

Even the risky business of fund-raisers and ticket sales exceeded expectations as the ASF's first Montgomery fund-raiser, "All the World's a Stage," sold out weeks in advance at $100 a ticket. The program featured an Italian juggler's version of "To Be or Not to Be," the Folger Consort, an Elizabethan fashion show featuring the Mayor of Montgomery, and a complete Elizabethan dinner donated by the Governors House, a local hotel and conference center.

And to the surprise of virtually everyone in the state, the ASF's Masterpiece Champagne Opening, featuring ten plays and the highest

Opening Gala volunteers led by Gala Chairman Peggy Mussafer (standing in background) prepare for the opening $1,000-per-person fund-raiser for the ASF endowment fund. (1985)

I am delighted to learn of the theatre which is being established in Montgomery, Alabama, through the generosity of Mr. and Mrs. Winton M. Blount to be the home of the Alabama Shakespeare Festival company. This exciting and imaginative initiative will I'm sure be welcomed by theatre lovers in this country and throughout America and I offer my very sincere good wishes for the success of the venture.

The Queen Mother

price tag of any theatre subscription in the State of Alabama, sold out within six weeks of the printing of the brochure!

It came as no surprise that the new home and fifteen-year-old reputation of the Alabama Shakespeare Festival attracted thousands of resumes and phone calls from interested individuals from throughout the United States and many foreign countries and aroused the volunteer instincts of hundreds of local citizens.

Staffing the New Theatre

"Welcome hither, As is the spring to the earth."

THE WINTER'S TALE

As part of its commitment to Alabama and the improvement of the local economy, the ASF dedicated itself to hiring on a regional basis in order to benefit from the experience and expertise of local professionals. The search immediately turned up Barbara Larson, a Montgomery native, as Director of Development; Eve Shearer of Montgomery, as Coordinator of Volunteer Services; Donni Cooper, a Montgomery resident, as Office Manager; Larry Stafford of Huntsville, as Group Sales Manager; M. P. Wilkerson of Montgomery, as Coordinator of Public Relations; Catherine Martin of Florence, as Telemarketing Manager; Simon Bovinett, an Auburn graduate, as the Assistant to the Director of Marketing; Richard Norris, an Auburn graduate, as Box Office Manager; and Stacy Coats of Montgomery, as Subscriptions Manager.

As part of the ASF's expansion, Doug Perry, ASF Business Manager, was promoted to General Manager. One of those rare theatre administrators who can balance a myriad of organizational activities as well as budgets, Perry seized a lot of the crucial day-to-day administrative work, freeing up the Executive Staff (Jim Volz and Martin L. Platt) to concentrate on special projects, Board of Director development, artistic and management strategies, and long-range planning.

Staff member Shiela Brantley prepares for intermission in front of a plaque honoring Winton M. and Carolyn Blount.

Will's Guild

One of the key special projects in Montgomery was the development of a large volunteer force—the backbone of all regional theatre operations. Local community leaders initially organized by Eve Shearer quickly drew up plans for volunteer support.

On March 21, 1985, a dozen members of an ASF steering committee met to discuss objectives, by-laws, and responsibilities of a potential Montgomery-based volunteer group. Perhaps the most important agenda item of the day was the selection of a new name for ASF volunteers in the capital city. Following consideration of such catchy labels as "Shakespeare's Shakers," "The Bard's Babes," and "Touchstone," the volunteers overwhelmingly decided on a guild of men *and* women and selected "Will's Guild" as the group's new title. Steering committee member Tootsie Emmet contributed the name and soon volunteers from throughout the area were answering the call to join Will's Guild.

The Grand Opening

The opening of the new home for the State Theatre sparked national interest as the premiere performances of *A Midsummer Night's Dream* on the Festival Stage and *The Glass Menagerie* in the Octagon thrilled audience members from throughout the United States. The Gala Week, December 6–13, 1985, combined the special previews, a week of parties, celebrations, and ribbon-cutting ceremonies.

With the opening of the new theatre, the Festival has the technical capability and a large enough company to do major plays such as *Richard III*, with 130 speaking roles. This season is also the first time the Festival has done a contemporary play, *Betrayal*, by controversial English playwright Harold Pinter.

Other plays in what Platt called "the most exciting season of comedy and drama offered by any theatre in America" are: *A Midsummer Night's Dream*, *The Merry Wives of Windsor*, *A Flea in Her Ear*, *Pygmalion*, *The School for Scandal*, and *Death of a Salesman*. *The Imaginary Heir*, by Jean-Francois Regnard, "represents a new direction for the Festival of rediscovering classic plays, successful in their own country, but not known to the English-speaking world," said Platt.

Fascinating Facts

Few theatregoers are aware of the labor-intensive nature of professional theatre. For example, on an annual basis, nearly 60,000 work hours go into each ASF season's costumes, shoes, boots, hats, and wigs.

In efforts to cut costs and assure good quality, the ASF employs nearly two dozen professional seamstresses, cutters, milliners, tailors, craftspeople, and cobblers.

Carpenters, metalworkers, and scene painters build the elaborate scenery, and this crew numbers between ten and twenty-four throughout the year. Another four to six artisans are employed in the properties shop. These talented individuals are responsible for the endless array of severed heads, swords, crowns, wagons, cannons, maps, and corpses that grace the stage in so many classical productions.

Over 550 lighting instruments are used to create special effects by lighting designers, and miles of cable snake through all parts of the building connecting the instruments to the modern computerized lighting control system in each theatre.

Most of the actors in the ASF productions are members of the Actors Equity Association, the professional actors union. These actors work in virtually all of the major theatres in America in addition to Broadway, off-Broadway, films, and television. The PAT/MFA (Professional Actor Training/Master of Fine Arts Program) students comprise the next largest group of actors in ASF productions; they fill in the smaller roles and work as understudies.

Did you know that the $21.5 million donation of the two-theatre complex marks one of the largest single gifts to a theatre company in the history of American giving? The Festival's $4 million annual operating budget also makes it one of the largest regional theatres in the United States. The Montgomery Area Chamber of Commerce projects the economic impact of the ASF at $11.2 million in direct and $90 million in indirect impact.

It may also be a little-known fact that the one-year leap from an $800,000 budget to a $4 million budget is one of the largest single expansions in the history of America's regional theatre movement. Contributions alone increased from $511,000 to over $2 million in the first year.

Record-Breaking Support

Within one year of moving into the new complex, the ASF mobilized hundreds of volunteers, over 30,000 students, all of the state's universities, hundreds of businesses and corporations, the city of Montgomery, the State Legislature, State Board of Education, State Arts Council, the Committee for the Humanities in Alabama, the National Endowment for the Arts, the National Endowment for the Humanities, and the State Bureau of Tourism and Travel in the promotion and/or support of the Festival's cultural and educational programs.

Given this remarkable support, few were surprised when the ASF set

ASF audiences more than tripled in the 1985-86 season, and sold-out houses were common throughout the premiere winter season.

The opening of the Alabama Shakespeare Festival at Wynfield marks the beginning of a new era of cultural sophistication and excellence for the great state of Alabama. The opening of this magnificent complex reflects the dedication and commitment of Alabamians to the highest standards in the arts and education. Mr. and Mrs. Blount's gift and the ongoing work of the Alabama Shakespeare Festival will shape lives in the South for generations to come.

George C. Wallace
Governor of Alabama

A Look to the Future   121

a new fourteen-year box office record within six weeks of the printing of the premiere winter season brochure. Nearly eight months prior to the ASF's first production, over a quarter of a million dollars worth of tickets had been sold—more than the total ticket sales for an entire season in previous years!

A Model for America

In terms of regional and national significance, the development of the Alabama Shakespeare Festival marks one of the most extensive and exciting theatre movements in America this decade. The scope of the expansion efforts includes the networking of hundreds of volunteers and civic leaders throughout Alabama; fund-raising from throughout the Southeast; consulting efforts from throughout the United States; the mobilization of over 35,000 students as part of the student matinee program; and over one million dollars in marketing efforts designed to touch the lives of millions throughout America and carefully targeted areas in the southern United States.

According to Governor George C. Wallace, "Alabama has taken many small steps in the performing arts in the last 25 to 30 years. Many of them have been unnoted. However, the biggest step is being taken by the Alabama Shakespeare Festival."

The growth of the Alabama Shakespeare Festival is significant on a nationwide basis for a number of reasons. As the only professional theatre in Alabama and one of the few classical repertory theatres in

Evelyn Carol Case, Bruce Cromer, Tom Rolfing, and Shannon Eubanks as the young lovers in the 1985–86 ASF production of A Midsummer Night's Dream.

America, the ASF is taking a bold step forward when many of the nation's theatres are struggling, retrenching, or simply falling by the wayside. The remarkable partnerships fostered by the ASF will hopefully serve as a model for other organizations threatened with extinction due to lack of support from the local or statewide community.

The Alabama State Legislature, the State Arts Council, the cities of Montgomery and Anniston, the county of Montgomery, and hundreds of businesses and corporations have all contributed in many ways to the ASF's well-being. The assistance of these many crucial civic, government, and business leaders has helped the ASF touch the lives of thousands of students, senior citizens, and countless other audience members in their own communities or in the ASF's home theatre. The cultural, educational, and economic impact of this historical partnership is difficult to pinpoint but generally understood by all involved.

The practical advantages and joys of the arts were eloquently stated by Representative Simon of Illinois in a speech before the entire House of Representatives:

> The reality is that arts are a help to the economy of this country. The reality is we are going to be remembered as a civilization someday not for the bombers we build or the tanks we make or the ribbons of concrete with which we sometimes brutalize the landscape. We are going to be remembered for other things. . . .

Joan Ulmer as Amanda in the 1985–86 drama, The Glass Menagerie.

An interior view of the ASF lobby and balcony in the new Montgomery complex.

Cultural support is an investment, returning far more to local economics than it costs. For example, for every $1 spent on cultural activities, at least $4 is spent on related activities such as transportation, lodging, and restaurants. A February, 1983, study of the New York area credited the arts with over 110,000 jobs and an infusion of $5.6 billion into the economy. Funding for the arts is good business and it is important to our spirit as a Nation.

The Alabama Shakespeare Festival is making a historic move toward achieving the goals that were first outlined in 1972. The unique and challenging mission is to present the classics with a resident company and to shed light on modern times by exploring Shakespeare and other brilliant playwrights as a vibrant, living part of our dramatic literature and heritage.

In the words of Artistic Director Platt:

> The vision of the future is that of a company dedicated to producing classical repertory theatre with a resident ensemble working together year-round to create a cohesive body of work. A theatre is the artistic vision of its director, which is collectively acted upon by the actors, designers, and other directors who work within the theatre. By developing an ensemble of actors, designers, and directors who can build a permanent base with the Festival, we can continue to evolve and build upon the work we have created throughout the past decade. Working with a permanent ensemble allows the work to develop. A resident company, committed to the theatre and whom the theatre is committed to, is relieved of the pressures of searching for work and free to explore and develop its art and craft.

Throughout the history of the ASF there has been a consistency in the artistic work and vision that has touched the lives of hundreds of thousands of theatregoers. When *The New York Times* labeled the ASF "brash and brilliant" in 1976, the company took great pride in its history and vision. However, when *The Washington Post* remarked in 1983 that Alabama's State Theatre was only in "the upper quarter of American regional theatres," it was clear that the Alabama Shakespeare Festival still had work to do.

ASF craftsman Sylvester Yunker welding scenery in preparation for the opening plays in the new theatres, 1985.

Regional and national press and friends from throughout the world gathered in Montgomery to dedicate the ASF complex on December 7, 1985.

A reporter interviews Carolyn Blount (center) and Thomas Blount (right) prior to the opening-day festivities in 1985.

Mayor Emory Folmar (left) leads the security forces for the Public Dedication of the Carolyn Blount Theatre.

Appendix A

HISTORICAL CHRONOLOGY

ALABAMA SHAKESPEARE FESTIVAL, THE STATE THEATRE

Fall, 1971	Beverly Hills native Martin L. Platt, Director of the Anniston Little Theatre, brainstorms idea for an Alabama Shakespeare Festival.
January, 1972	First ASF season announced to public: *Hamlet, The Comedy of Errors, The Two Gentlemen of Verona,* and *Hedda Gabler.* Single tickets are set at $2 with season subscriptions available for $7.50.
Spring, 1972	ASF receives its first government grant from the Alabama State Council on the Arts and Humanities.
Spring, 1972	Mrs. George C. (Cornelia) Wallace is appointed Honorary President of the ASF Board of Governors.
July 10, 1972	Mrs. Thomas Potts hosts first meeting of area volunteers who will later form the crucial ASF Guild.
July 12, 1972	*The Comedy of Errors* opens the first ASF season in the unair-conditioned old Anniston High School gymnasium.
1973	B. C. Moore appointed first President of the ASF Board of Directors.
August 1, 1973	The ASF Guild is officially christened with Mrs. Thomas Potts elected President.
July 12, 1973	*Much Ado About Nothing* opens the second ASF season in the new 1,000-seat Anniston Educational Complex.
1974	William J. Davis is appointed President of the ASF Board of Directors.
July 19, 1974	*A Midsummer Night's Dream* opens the ASF's third season. The ASF receives national press for the first time as *The National Observer* writes: "The Bard would have approved."
1975	The new high school auditorium is officially renamed "The Festival Theatre."
July 19, 1975	*The Tempest* opens the ASF's fourth season, and *Ralph Roister Doister* premieres as the first "apprentice" production.
1975	The ASF Junior Guild of young lady volunteers is created with Griffin Doster as president.
1976	Josephine E. Ayers appointed President of ASF Board.
	After sixteen previous ASF productions and five years, Martin

"There is a history in all men's lives."

HENRY IV, PART TWO

L. Platt hires the ASF's first guest director, Bruce Hoard, who directs *The Merry Wives of Windsor*.

ASF hires its first professional actor, Charles Antalosky, to play King Lear, Falstaff, Camillo, and Harpagon.

A new stage floor and scenic concept is devised by Robert Moeller. Single tickets skyrocket to $4 and $2.

July 17, 1976	*The Winter's Tale* opens the fifth ASF season. *The New York Times* review of the season describes the ASF as "brash and brilliant."
1977	Anne Zimmerman joins the ASF as the first full-time administrator to head operations as Managing Director.
June 17, 1977	Governor George C. Wallace proclaims the Alabama Shakespeare Festival "The State Theatre of Alabama."
July 15, 1977	ASF repeats its first play with a second production of *Hamlet*.
July 23, 1977	ASF presents its first work by a living playwright, producing *Rosencrantz and Guildenstern Are Dead* by Tom Stoppard.

The Foundation for the Extension and Development of the American Professional Theatre (FEDAPT) selects the ASF for membership in the administrative counseling program.

1977	ASF audiences increase by 52 percent to over 15,000.
1978	A new stage is designed by Michael Stauffer.

ASF income doubles in one year, breaking a quarter of a million dollars for the first time.

A major student conservatory program is kicked off at the ASF with ten young actors enrolled.

October, 1978	*The Taming of the Shrew* launches the ASF's first major touring venture, traveling to seven states in six weeks. A classical film series is instituted for home audiences.

ASF helps the City of Anniston win the coveted All-America City Award. The Board of Directors sponsors the first Opening Night Gala.

Josephine E. Ayers is named Executive Producer of ASF.

1979	ASF acting company grows to forty-two. *As You Like It* headlines the Festival's eighth anniversary season.

Philip Pleasants grandstands before the Alabama Legislature in their executive chamber in the ASF production of *Clarence Darrow*.

"Shakespeare Sundays," the ASF's popular Elizabethan Church Services, are instituted as part of the Festival.

ASF Tour of *Twelfth Night* reaches out to over 30,000 theatregoers in eleven states.

1980	Michael Maso is hired as ASF's second Managing Director. A fifth major production is added to the ASF roster for the first time. The budget exceeds a half million dollars, and the ASF's first major financial problems begin to surface.
	The popular "Music at St. Michael's" series is created, and the ASF Madrigal Singers debut as part of the series. The League of Resident Theatres (LORT) invites the ASF to join their ranks.
1981	A second theatre is added to the ASF, and the musical *Oh, Coward!* opens the ACT Playhouse in downtown Anniston. *Oh, Coward!* is the ASF's first full musical and marked the Festival's first production in Atlanta, Georgia.
	ASF expenses rise 31 percent to over three quarters of a million dollars, creating major deficits and endangering the Festival's financial and institutional stability.
	"A Midsummer Morn's Run," a 3.1-mile event written up in *Runner's World,* helps the ASF celebrate its tenth anniversary season.
1982	*Red Fox/Second Hangin'* and *Junebug Jabbo Jones* are booked into the ACT Playhouse, marking the first time the ASF books in shows on subscription.
May, 1982	Negotiations begin between the Blount Foundation and the Alabama Shakespeare Festival to solve financial problems.
July 13, 1982	The ASF's proposed expansion to year-round operations in a new Montgomery-based complex donated by Winton M. "Red" and Carolyn Blount is unveiled to the public.
January, 1983	Jim Volz joins the ASF as its third Managing Director.
April, 1983	"Shakespeare's Birthday Party" is devised as an annual Elizabethan fund-raiser.
June 1, 1983	A "Shakespeare Bill" passes the Alabama Legislature allowing a nonprofit authority to issue bonds and construct facilities to house the ASF.
1983	Winton and Carolyn Blount unveil plans to construct an exact replica of Shakespeare's birthplace as an addition to the grounds where the theatre complex is to be constructed.
	John E. Kelly is elected the fourth Chairman of the ASF Board of Directors.
	ASF produces its first American play, *Mass Appeal,* by Bill C. Davis.
	Richard Coe of *The Washington Post* describes the ASF as "in at least the upper quarter of American regional theatres."
	Carol Ogus, Director of ASF Touring Programs, kicks off the ASF's first major artist-in-education programs.

"My dreams presage some joyful news at hand."

ROMEO AND JULIET

November, 1983	The ASF's 1983 production of *Mass Appeal* is transferred to Indianapolis's Indiana Repertory Theatre for a highly successful sold-out run.
	"Shakespeare: Theatre in the Mind," a joint project of the ASF and the Committee for the Humanities in Alabama is funded nearly $75,000 by the National Endowment for the Humanities. Shakespeare seminars are set up in eighteen Alabama communities. International theatre director Jonathan Miller is scheduled to visit the ASF in 1984.
December, 1983	ASF breaks the one-million-dollar mark in income for the first time in its history as income rises 51 percent in one year.
1984	The Alabama State Legislature conditionally appropriates $750,000 to the ASF, marking one of the largest state appropriations for theatre operational support in U.S. history.
February, 1984	The Consortium for Academic Programs in association with the Alabama Shakespeare Festival, envisioned as a vehicle for promoting the mutual interests of the state's academic community and the ASF, meets at Auburn University. Dr. Guin A. Nance, Auburn University at Montgomery, is elected President of the Consortium.
Spring, 1984	Juliette Doster and John Kelly spearhead major fund-raising efforts, and the citizens of Calhoun County raise over $172,000 to "Save the 1984 Anniston Season" and replace costumes destroyed in a disastrous fire set by thieves earlier in the year.
August, 1984	A major concert series is launched at the ASF, featuring the Birmingham Heritage Band and the Atlanta Chamber Players. Monteverdi's Vespers of 1610 is featured in the "Music at St. Michael's" series. *Billy Bishop Goes to War, Love's Labour's Lost, Macbeth, She Stoops to Conquer,* and *Oh, Mr. Faulkner, Do You Write?* round out the Festival's last full summer season in Anniston, Alabama.

MOVING DAY—*the ASF staff's first day in the new Montgomery complex! (September 1985)*

Fall, 1984	ASF moves its base of operations to Montgomery, Alabama, to temporary offices in Executive Park.
	ASF tours *Arms and the Man* throughout the southeastern U.S.A.
Winter, 1985	ASF leads patrons on an international theatre trip to London, Paris, Stratford-on-Avon, Versailles, and Chartres.
	Philip A. Sellers is elected the ASF's fifth Chairman of the Board of Directors.
Spring, 1985	"All the World's a Stage," ASF's first Montgomery fund-raiser, features The Folger Consort and sells out weeks in advance.
Summer, 1985	Arts Council support for $80,000 in ticket subsidies for Alabama students attending ASF productions and Committee for the Humanities funding for "Shakespeare: Theatre in the Mind" solidifies statewide partnership.
Fall, 1985	Students begin study and training in the new MFA Professional Actor Training Program, which cements a firm liaison between the University of Alabama, the Consortium for Academic Programs, and the ASF.
December 6–12, 1985	Gala Week for the ASF's premiere winter season in Montgomery draws friends from throughout the nation.
December, 1985	Defying superstition, *A Midsummer Night's Dream* opens the ASF's new Festival Stage on Friday the 13th! *The Glass Menagerie* opens the Octagon.
1986	The ASF's first year-long season features thirteen plays, over twenty musical events, and a myriad of special programs, lectures, and seminars.

"Be not afraid of greatness: some are born great, some achieve greatness and some have greatness thrust upon them."

TWELFTH NIGHT

Left to right: Barbara Larson, Carolyn Blount, and Eve Shearer at the first company meeting in the new ASF complex, November 1985.

CHRONOLOGY OF ASF PLAYS, AUDIENCE STATISTICS, AND BUDGETS

YEAR	AUTHOR	DIRECTOR	THEATRE
1972			
The Comedy of Errors	Shakespeare	Martin L. Platt	Festival Playhouse
Hamlet	Shakespeare	Martin L. Platt	Festival Playhouse
Hedda Gabler	Henrik Ibsen	Martin L. Platt	Festival Playhouse
The Two Gentlemen of Verona	Shakespeare	Martin L. Platt	Festival Playhouse

Summer Attendance: 3,000   **Total Expenses:** 8,000   **Total Income:** 7,966

YEAR	AUTHOR	DIRECTOR	THEATRE
1973			
As You Like It	Shakespeare	Martin L. Platt	Festival Playhouse
Macbeth	Shakespeare	Martin L. Platt	Festival Playhouse
Much Ado About Nothing	Shakespeare	Martin L. Platt	Festival Playhouse
Tartuffe	Molière	Martin L. Platt	Festival Playhouse

Mark Loigman presenting plans for the ASF's first Montgomery season.

Summer Attendance: 5,000   **Total Expenses:** 23,890   **Total Income:** 21,100

YEAR	AUTHOR	DIRECTOR	THEATRE
1974			
A Midsummer Night's Dream	Shakespeare	Martin L. Platt	Festival Playhouse
Romeo and Juliet	Shakespeare	Martin L. Platt	Festival Playhouse
The Taming of the Shrew	Shakespeare	Martin L. Platt	Festival Playhouse
The School for Wives	Molière	Martin L. Platt	Festival Playhouse
Mandragola	Machiavelli	Bruce Hoard	Festival Playhouse

Summer Attendance: 7,000   **Total Expenses:** 32,140   **Total Income:** 42,005

YEAR	AUTHOR	DIRECTOR	THEATRE
1975			
Fitting for Ladies	Georges Feydeau	Martin L. Platt	Festival Playhouse

YEAR	AUTHOR	DIRECTOR	THEATRE
Richard II	Shakespeare	Martin L. Platt	Festival Playhouse
The Tempest	Shakespeare	Martin L. Platt	Festival Playhouse
Twelfth Night	Shakespeare	Martin L. Platt	Festival Playhouse
Ralph Roister Doister	Nicholas Udall	Bruce Hoard	Festival Playhouse

Total Attendance: 10,000

Total Expenses:	50,466
Total Income:	48,862

"Play out the play."

HENRY IV, PART ONE

1976

King Lear	Shakespeare	Martin L. Platt	Festival Playhouse
The Merry Wives of Windsor	Shakespeare	Bruce Hoard	Festival Playhouse
The Miser	Molière	Martin L. Platt	Festival Playhouse
The Winter's Tale	Shakespeare	Martin L. Platt	Festival Playhouse

Summer Attendance: 10,000

Total Expenses:	77,550
Total Income:	85,239

1977

Hamlet	Shakespeare	Martin L. Platt	Festival Playhouse
The Hollow Crown	John Barton	Martin L. Platt and Bruce Hoard	Festival Playhouse
The Imaginary Invalid	Molière	Martin L. Platt	Festival Playhouse
Love's Labour's Lost	Shakespeare	Martin L. Platt	Festival Playhouse
Rosencrantz and Guildenstern Are Dead	Tom Stoppard	Martin L. Platt	Festival Playhouse

Summer Attendance: 15,000

Total Expenses:	125,444
Total Income:	114,721

Olivia deHavilland, Lord and Lady Wright, Caspar and Jane Weinberger, and Winton M. and Carolyn Blount at the dedication of the new ASF complex.

An Edwardian A Midsummer Night's Dream *at ASF|in 1985–86.*

Joan Ulmer as Amanda in the ASF's first production in the new Octagon theatre, The Glass Menagerie.

Joan Ulmer as Amanda in the 1986 ASF tour of The Glass Menagerie.

Patricia Boyette, Joan Ulmer, and Robert Browning in the 1985–86 drama, The Glass Menagerie.

YEAR	AUTHOR	DIRECTOR	THEATRE
1978			
Clarence Darrow	David W. Rintels	Martin L. Platt	Festival Playhouse
A Lover's Complaint	Martin L. Platt	Martin L. Platt	Festival Playhouse
Measure for Measure	Shakespeare	Martin L. Platt	Festival Playhouse
The Merchant of Venice	Shakespeare	Martin L. Platt	Festival Playhouse
Othello	Shakespeare	Martin L. Platt	Festival Playhouse
Private Lives	Sir Noel Coward	Fred Chappell	Festival Playhouse
The Taming of the Shrew	Shakespeare	Martin L. Platt	Touring Production

Summer Attendance: 23,000
Tour Attendance: 22,000
Total Expenses: 252,374
Total Income: 253,227

1979			
As You Like It	Shakespeare	Martin L. Platt	Festival Playhouse
Clarence Darrow	David W. Rintels	Martin L. Platt	Festival Playhouse
The Comedy of Errors	Shakespeare	Russell Treyz	Festival Playhouse
The Country Wife	Wycherley	Martin L. Platt	Festival Playhouse
Oh, William!	Russell Treyz and Martin L. Platt	Russell Treyz	Festival Playhouse
Twelfth Night	Shakespeare	Martin L. Platt	Touring Production

Summer Attendance: 24,000
Tour Attendance: 40,000
Total Expenses: 410,694
Total Income: 409,197

1980			
Cymbeline	Shakespeare	Martin L. Platt	Festival Playhouse
The Importance of Being Earnest	Oscar Wilde	Martin L. Platt	Festival Playhouse
Romeo and Juliet	Shakespeare	Martin L. Platt	Festival Playhouse
Tartuffe	Molière	Russell Treyz	Festival Playhouse
The Two Gentlemen of Verona	Shakespeare	Russell Treyz	Festival Playhouse

Summer Attendance: 25,500
Tour Attendance: 40,000
Total Expenses: 542,449
Total Income: 505,873

Wigs for the ASF are made and fashioned in the ASF costume shop (1985).

YEAR	AUTHOR	DIRECTOR	THEATRE
1981			
Henry IV, Part One	Shakespeare	Martin L. Platt	Festival Playhouse
A Mid-summer Night's Dream	Shakespeare	Martin L. Platt	Festival Playhouse
Much Ado About Nothing	Shakespeare	Jay Broad	Festival Playhouse
Oh, Coward!	Sir Noel Coward	Judith Haskell	ACT Theatre
Servant of Two Mas-ters	Carlo Goldoni	Martin L. Platt	Festival Playhouse
The Marowitz Hamlet	Charles Marowitz	Jim Donadio	Conservatory Play
The Impor-tance of Being Earnest	Oscar Wilde	Martin L. Platt	Touring Produc-tion

Summer Attendance: 26,000
Tour Attendance: 25,000

Total Expenses: 785,887
Total Income: 736,098

YEAR	AUTHOR	DIRECTOR	THEATRE
1982			
Hamlet	Shakespeare	Martin L. Platt	Festival Playhouse
Junebug Jabbo Jones	John O'Neal	Curtis King	ACT Theatre
Red Fox/ Second Hangin'	Dudley Cocke and Don Baker	Roadside Theatre	ACT Theatre
Uncle Vanya	Anton Chekhov	Martin L. Platt	Festival Playhouse
The Comedy of Errors	Shakespeare	John-Frederick Jones	Conservatory Play
Twelfth Night	Shakespeare	Sanford Robbins	Festival Playhouse
Romeo and Juliet	Shakespeare	Martin L. Platt	Touring Produc-tion

Summer Attendance: 21,400
Tour Attendance: 33,000

Total Expenses: 694,769
Total Income: 677,161

General Manager Doug Perry reviews policy at the ASF's first full company meeting in Montgomery, November 1985.

YEAR	AUTHOR	DIRECTOR	THEATRE
1983			
All's Well That Ends Well	Shakespeare	Martin L. Platt	Festival Playhouse
Arms and the Man	Bernard Shaw	Martin L. Platt	Festival Playhouse
King Lear	Shakespeare	Martin L. Platt	Festival Playhouse
Mass Appeal	Bill Davis	Martin L. Platt	ACT Theatre
The Taming of the Shrew	Shakespeare	Craig Belknap	Festival Playhouse
Love's Labour's Lost	Shakespeare	John-Frederick Jones	Conservatory Play
The Comedy of Errors	Shakespeare	John-Frederick Jones	Touring Production

Summer Attendance: 23,400

Tour Attendance: 33,000

Total Expenses: 759,685

Total Income: 1,024,604

ASF staff, Alabama Humanities Foundation staff, and university leaders meet to plan educational programs as part of the 1985–86 ASF season.

Educational Services Director Carol Ogus contemplating plans for ASF's SchoolFest, "Theatre in the Mind," and ASF on Tour in 1986.

YEAR	AUTHOR	DIRECTOR	THEATRE
1984			
Billy Bishop Goes to War	John Gray	Charles Abbott	ACT Theatre
Love's Labour's Lost	Shakespeare	Martin L. Platt	Festival Playhouse
Macbeth	Shakespeare	Martin L. Platt	Festival Playhouse
Oh, Mr. Faulkner, Do You Write?	John Maxwell with Tom Dupree	William Partlan	ACT Theatre
She Stoops to Conquer	Oliver Goldsmith	Martin L. Platt	Festival Playhouse
Arms and the Man	Bernard Shaw	Martin L. Platt	Touring Production

Summer Attendance: 25,000
Tour Attendance: 36,000
Educational Programs: 9,000

Total Expenses: 792,677
Total Income: 836,867

YEAR	AUTHOR	DIRECTOR	THEATRE
1985–1986			
A Midsummer Night's Dream	Shakespeare	Martin L. Platt	Festival Stage
The Merry Wives of Windsor	Shakespeare	Tony Van Bridge	Festival Stage
Richard III	Shakespeare	Ed Stern	Festival Stage
Death of a Salesman	Arthur Miller	Ed Stern	Festival Stage
Pygmalion	Bernard Shaw	Martin L. Platt	Festival Stage
A Flea in Her Ear	Georges Feydeau	Martin L. Platt	Festival Stage
The School for Scandal	Richard Brinsley Sheridan	Russell Treyz	Festival Stage
The Glass Menagerie	Williams	Russell Treyz	The Octagon
The Imaginary Heir	Regnard	Martin L. Platt	The Octagon
Betrayal	Harold Pinter	Martin L. Platt	The Octagon

Philip A. Sellers, Martin Platt, Mayor Folmar, Tony Randall, and Lady Flower prepare to speak at the ASF dedication. Lady Flower, a special guest from Stratford, England, presented special greetings and a gift from the Royal Shakespeare Company.

I bring greetings from Stratford-on-Avon, the birthplace of William Shakespeare. This theatre surpasses everything. . . . I'm going to be very cautious, Englishmen always are—it's the finest theatre complex and setting anywhere, anyplace, anytime.

Dennis Flower
Chairman of the Board
Royal Shakespeare Company
Stratford, England

Appendix C

ASF HISTORICAL PERSONNEL LISTING

EXECUTIVE STAFF

Martin L. Platt
Artistic Director, 1972–Present

Jim Volz
Managing Director, 1982–Present

Josephine E. Ayers
Executive Producer, 1978–1982

Michael Maso
Managing Director, 1980–1982

Anne F. Zimmerman
Managing Director, 1977–1979

ARTISTIC STAFF

Charles Abbott	Donald Lee Green	Judy Rasmuson
Paul Ackerman	Matthew Greenbaum	Susan M. Rheaume
Richard Andrew	Lori Grifo	Arlene Ritz
Alan Armstrong	Judith Haskell	Sanford Robbins
Dr. John Arthos	Byron Hays	Philip Rosenberg
Normand L. Beauregard	Cassandra Henning	John Ross
Allen R. Belknap	Sydney Hibbert	Anne Sandoe
Patricia Boyette	Bruce Hoard	Lester Shane
Jay Broad	Michael P. Howley	Michael Stauffer
Robert Browning	Dr. Charles Johnson	Don Steffy
Michael Burt	John-Frederick Jones	Ed Stern
Col. Robert Byrom	Margaret Jones	Joel Stoehr
Evelyn Carol Case	Philipp Jung	David Strohauer
Fred Chappell	Kris Kearney	Melissa Taylor
Marydith Chase	Charles J. Kilian, Jr.	James Thorp
Joe Collins	Sam Kirkpatrick	Peter Jack Tkatch
Tom Cone	Bill Leonard	Gwendolyn Toth
Jim Conely	Ann Mathews	Russell Treyz
Susan A. Cox	Susan E. Mickey	Paul Valoris
Louise Crofton	Lauren Mackenzie Miller	Tony Van Bridge
Bruce B. Cromer	Alvin Moeller	Jim Volz
James Donadio	Bob Moeller	Patrick Watkins
James Eckhouse	Timothy Monich	Michael Watson
Lynne Emmert	Jane Moore	Mary White
Shannon Eubanks	Mark Morton	Myron White
Phillip A. Evola	April Parke	Edmond Williams
Michael Fauss	William Partlan	Susan Willis
Lynn Fitzpatrick	Martin L. Platt	Edrian Winters

ACTORS

Edwin Abernathy	Daniel Dean Armitage	Alvin Balin
Carol Allin	David N. Asbell	Jaclyn Barnhart
Alan Almeida	Ethan Auslander	Andrew Barnicle
Richard Andrew	Ann Bainbridge	Dennis Bateman
Charles Antalosky	Don Baker	Karen Bauder

"The best actors in the world, either for tragedy, comedy, history."

HAMLET

Barbara Beatty-Shrawder
Terry Beaver
Don Bednarz
Janet Belcher
Allison Biggers
Leslie Blake
Robert Bloodworth
Patricia Boyette
Ed Braden
Lisa Brailoff
Billie Brenan
Cathy Brewer-Moore
Zander Brietzke
Kathy Brinton
Tom Brooks
Anthony Brown
Kermit Brown
Morris Brown
Robert Browning
Gayle Brownlee
Beaumont Bruestle
Dianne Burch
Jana Burroughs
Michael Burt
Rick Byquist
J. Wilkinson Cady
Pat Caffey
Dara Caldwell
Michael Caldwell
Cusi Campbell
Jean Campbell
James Canada
Theresa A. Carver
Evelyn Carol Case
Ida Caserta
Beulah Casey
Karen Casteel
Kathy Chandler
Christopher Clavelli
Quinton Cockrell
Andrew Cole
Rob Cole
Bruce Collier
Edward Conery
Stefan Cotner
James Cotten
A. D. Cover
Robert Cox
Jean Crean
Bruce Cromer
Kim Crow
Ron Culbreth
Joe DeBevc
Andre Degas
Kathryn Dell
Scott Depoy

James Donadio
Daryl Donley
Mark Douglas-Jones
James Eckhouse
Earle Edgerton
Marlene Egan
Robert Egan
Alice Elliott
Grant Elliott
Shannon Eubanks
Elaine Evans
Matthew Faison
Michele Farr
Deborah Fezelle
Larry Fishman
Ellen Fiske
Lynn Fitzpatrick
Carmen Flowers
Kathleen Forbes
William Forward
Patrick J. Frederic
LaFain Freeman
Sheree Galpert
Anne Geery
Thomas Gibson
Michael Gifford
William Grange
Larry E. Greer
Richard Grupenhoff
Lorenzo Gunn
Donna Haley
Arthur Hanket
Jacob Harran
Carol Haynes
Byron Hays
John Heider
James Helsinger
Elizabeth Henderson
Jim Hensleigh
Sydney Hibbert
Bruce Hoard
William Hollinde
George Holmes
Henry House
Charles Hutchins
Kate Ingram
Tad Ingram
Daniel Izzo
Rhonda Jackson
Miller James
William Todd Jeffries
Bill Jenkins
Mary Ann Jesse
Marcia Johnson
Ridge Johnson
John-Frederick Jones

Marilyn Jones
Mark Douglas Jones
Wendy Kaufman
William Kelly
Anne Kerr
Tom Key
Joseph King
David Meaders Klein
Lauren Koslow
David Krasner
Denise Krueger
Jack Kyrieleison
Bruce H. Laks
Greta Lambert
Carole Lampru
Sean Lancaster
David Landon
Dickson Lane
Judy Langford
Joseph Larrea
Jody Laurin
Deborah LaVine
Terry Layman
Paul LeBlanc
Evan Lee
Lissa LeGrand
Sharyn Leibman
Betty Leighton
Richard Levine
David Licht
Lawrence Lippert
Michael Lippert
David Locey
Randye Lordon
Paige Love
David M. Lowry
Lynn Lowry
Charles David Macaule
Jason McAuliffe
Beverly McBride
David McCann
Erik McConnell
William McHale
Michael McKenzie
Dennis McLernon
Howard McMaster
Lisa McMillan
Lester Malizia
Lilene Mansell
Rich Marlow
Ed Marona
Brian Martin
Judith Marx
Sandy Massie
Joseph Mauck
John Maxwell

Hunter May
Nicky Miller
Robert Miller II
William Miller
John Milligan
DeVora Millman
Cornelia Mills
Sean Mims
Jeffery Moody
Timothy Mooney
Andrew Moore
Catherine Moore
Jane Moore
Muriel Moore
Tricia Morgan
John W. Morrow, Jr.
Joseph Mullin
Margery Murray
Michael Myers
Joe Naftel
David Nava
Norman Neil
George Newman, Jr.
Douglas R. Nielsen
Michael O'Brien
Malia Ondrejka
Stuart O'Steen
Ned Osterhoff
Owen Page
Drew Penick
David Peterson
Harvey Phillips
Kerry Phillips
Steve Pickering
Autry Pinson
Philip Pleasants
Patricia Porter
Annemarie E. Potter
Steve Powers
Alan Prendergast
Sally W. Pressly
William Preston
Monte Priddy
Rosemary Prinz
Darcy Pulliam
Frank Raiter

Tom Reidy
Sebastian Richards
Gary Richardson
Robert Rieben
James Gray Riley
Robin Robinson
Tom Rolfing
Clarinda Ross
Clay Rouse
Bobbi Dale Rowe
Russell Rowe
James Rugino
Richard Ruskell
Sebastian Russ
Doris Ryan
Kathleen Mary Sacchi
Charles E. Sanders
Anne Sandoe
Sam Sandoe
Mary Nell Santacroce
Claude-Albert Saucier
Janine Saxe
Robert Schalau, Jr.
Elizabeth Schuette
Lester Shane
Gregory Shroeder
Douglas Simes
Jennet Sinclair
Sharon Skinner
Pat Skipper
Tony Slez, Jr.
Darrell Smith
Delane Smith
Ty Smith
Hank Snider
Scott Snively
Mary Jo Sodd
Ronald Stanley Sopyla
Dawn Spare
Gary Stamp
Mike Stedham
Linda Stephens
Jean Sterrett
Douglas Stewart
Fiona Stewart
Ian Stulberg

J. Allen Suddeth
Steven Sutherland
Beth Taffee
Frank Taylor
Melissa Taylor
Randall Taylor
Richard Taylor
Danny Teal
Paul Thomas
James Thorp
Drew Tillotson
Tipper
Peter Jack Tkatch
Ronn Tombaugh
Robert C. Torri
George Trahanis
Richard Travis
Ralph Tropf
Joan Ulmer
Mark Varian
Jennifer Varner
William Verdeber
Ed Vincent
Greg Vines
Richard Voigts
Valerie Von Volz
Clint Vriezelaar
Ronald Wainscott
Patrick Watkins
Stuart Weems
Jack Wetherall
David Wheeler
Brian Whitney
Laura Whyte
Tom Whyte
Gaye Williams
Cal Winn
Steve Wise
Wayne Wofford
Darron Wright
Linda Yerina
Ken Young
David Zinn
Jerri Zoochi

"Prepare for mirth, for mirth becomes a feast."

PERICLES

Left: Thomas Hinds and the Montgomery Symphony perform on the veranda of the Carolyn Blount Theatre.

Right: Special Scottish performers entertain the public in front of the box office pavilion of the Carolyn Blount Theatre.

"Every man to his business."

William P. Acker
James Adams
Sandra G. Adams
Kerry K. Akstin
Helen Allen
Janie Allred
Glenn Andrews, Jr.
Maria Arnold
Laura Aubele
Ben Baker
Dana Bender
Jayetta Benefield
Claire Black
Matt Bliss
Steven Robert Bloom
Esther Bloomfield
Simon Bovinett
Ann E. Boylan
Shiela Brantley
Lola Bright
Richard Bush
Margaret Butcher
Margaret Byrd
Marla Canfield
John Carlisle
Margaret Carlisle
Nancy Carmichael
Beulah Casey
Kathy Chandler
Stacey Cheatham
Mary Ellen Chenette
Judy Clark
Scott Clark
Mary Katherine Clarke
Stacy Coats
Robert Coker
Becky Condray
Benjamin Condray
Anne Conely
David Conely
Donni Cooper
Steve Cornwell
Joseph Cowperthwaite
Elizabeth Cox
Patricia Crotty
Amy Crysel
Barbara Crysel
Charslyn Davis
William J. Davis
Kathy Dell
Marsha Coleman Doege
Michael Doege
James Donadio

Jay Drury
Ernie Eldredge
Ken Elkins
Laura Fessenden
Becky Fuller
Jamie Gallagher
Mimi Gallagher
Terry L. Gargus
Margaret Goolsby
Donald R. Goodman
Lori Grifo
Beth Gunnels
Jerry Harris
Bernice Harrison
Herb Hester
Harrison Hicks
Keren L. Hill
Jennifer Hubbard
Charles Hudson
Danny Hurt
Gaye Jeffers
Julian Jenkins
Kevin Jones
Margaret Jones
DeDee Jumper
Glenda E. Knight
Cookie Knott
Eileen Knott
Richard L. Kuroski
Lynda Lancaster
Barbara Larson
Wayne Larson
Patricia Lavender
Sammy Ledbetter
Chuck Lewis
Dina Lewis
Kay Locey
Ron Lock
Krista Long
Susan Looney
Rex E. Luker
Ron McCall
Terrell McCallister
Deanna McConnell
Tommy McConnell
Donna McCowan
Michael McKee
Donna McKenna-Smith
Michelle McKiernan
Debbie McMillan
Ken McNeil
Eleanor Maher
Kevin Marshall

April Martin
Catherine Martin
Kim Montgomery
Virginia Mooney
Catherine Moore
Kathy Morace
Mrs. Dorothy Morgan
Cynthia M. Murphree
Gail Murphree
Richard Norris
Carol Ogus
Joseph Osborne
Michael Overton
Cathleen Owens
Harriet Owens
Julie Pace
Bradley Page
Doug Perry
Stan Pippin
Martin L. Platt
Angela Dawn Pope
Sally Redding
Melanie Reeder
Ken Rhudy
James P. Richardson
Annette Robertson
Laura Ellen Rome
Eben Rose
Alexine Saunders
Eve Shearer
Michael Shears
Dan Shephard
Glenn Sizemore
Rosalyn Skipper
Barbara Smith
Cindy C. Smith
Katherine Paige Smith
Louis Sohn
Lynda Speaks
Bert Spence
Cyndi Sprayberry
Debbie Stachulak
Larry Stafford
Mike Stedham
Paul Straus
Amy Sweeney
Ellen B. Tisdale
Michael K. Trawick
Linda Tucker
Caroline Turner
Marian Uhlman
Jim Volz
Pat F. Waldorf

Susan Weiss	Tim Williams	Cynthia Wraight
Robert Whartenby	David Wills	Tony Yardley
Robert Stanley White	Cameron Wilson	Alice Young
Christin Whittington	Julia Wilson	Ken Young
M. P. Wilkerson	Chuck Woodall	
Frances Williams	Mrs. Jean Woodall	

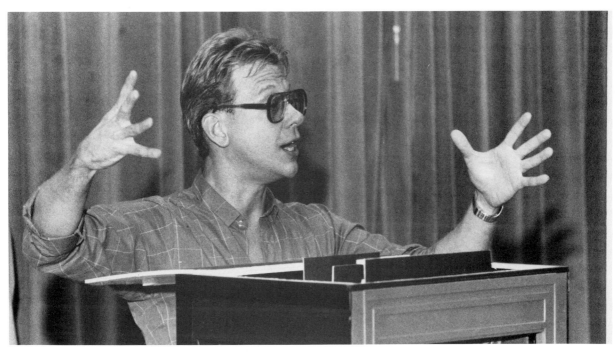

Above: ASF Designer Michael Stauffer explaining the design concept of A Midsummer Night's Dream *with the aid of a miniaturized model of the set.*

December 7, 1985 (Opening Day in the new complex). This is a great day for Alabama. Our thanks go to "Red" and Carolyn Blount and to everyone who has made this theatre possible. On behalf of the Board of Directors, I would like to publicly recognize and thank Blount/Pittman and Associated Architects, Inc. The care and attention that they have invested in all aspects of this building, from the magnificent sweeping exterior to the breathtaking beauty of the theatres make this theatre complex second to none. It inspires us in our creativity.

           Philip A. Sellers
           Chairman
           ASF Board of Directors

ASF dramaturg Susan Willis works on the "Theatre in the Mind" educational program.

"Tis not sleepy business."

CYMBELINE

Patricia Adams	Thom Coates	Pamela Guion
Judy Adamson	Steve Cobb	Brian Hager
Kerry Akstin	Pat Cochran	Kris Haglund
Eloise Albrecht	Lori Lee Coleman	Patricia Haldeman
Carol Allin	Christine A. Cook	Mark Halpin
Alan Allinger	Ron Cook	Leah Harris
Bill Andrews	Kate Corbley	Eric Harriz
David N. Asbell	Deborah Coutts	Judith Hart
Ethan Auslander	John A. Cowan	Rod Harter
Karen Baldwin	Lorraine Crane	Carol Haynes
Alvin Balin	Kyle Crew	Richard Haynes
Libby Ball	Rob Daughtry	Mary Anne Hempe
Bill Barksdale	Kathryn Dell	Jimmy Hensleigh
Jaclyn Barnhart	Hilda Dent	Tim Hester
John Bates	Pierre DeRagon	Thomas J. Hickey
Sandy Bates	Douglas DeVille	Brenda Hill
Angela Lynn Batey	Eileen DeVille	Sam Hitchcock
Jeff Baughn	Sherrill deWitt-Howard	Bruce Hoard
Deb Baxter	Will Dobson	Betty Jane Hutchison
Hi Bedford	Anne Doherty	Howard Tim Irish
Donna Bell	Pat Doty	Kay Jennings
Jeanne Berger	Jon Drtina	James Jensen
Allison Biggers	Paula Drucker	Larry Johnson
Rebecca Binks	Irene Duffner	Bill Jones
Blaise Box	Denise Dugas	Gary Jones
Kathleen Boyette	Amelia Dyer	Laura Jones
Ed Braden	Karen E. Edwards	Wendy Juren
Bill Bradford	Margo Elkow	Debby Kaufer
Peg Brady	Lynne Emmert	Rebecca Kaufman
Kathleen Brancato	Rose Mary Etheridge	Juantia Kaylor
Jerry Brenner	Phillip A. Evola	Kristine A. Kearney
Colleen Bresnahan	Gary W. Fassler	Sally A. Kessler
Alexander Brietzke	Laurence Feldman	Charles J. Kilian, Jr.
Richard Bristow	Jeff Fender	John Kiriakos
Owen Brooks	Carol Rae Fisher	Dena Kirkland
Frederick T. Brown	Philip J. Fleming	Bill Knapp
Greg Brown	Thomas J. Floeter	Nancy Knott
Philip Brown	Lee Foster	Lorin Knouse
Deborah Brunson	Roger Foster	Jacquie Konzen
Beth Buchanan	Jeff Frazier	Kristen R. Kuipers
Carol Buell	Christopher Fretts	T. C. La Biche
Deborah Bunson	Steve Frye	Michael Lackey
Beth Burgess	Sandra Fuller	Carole Lampru
William D. Buxton	Anne Geery	Dickson Lane
Margaret Byrd	Donna Gessell	Don Laney
T. J. Campbell	Brenda S. Gibson	Jody Laurin
Dante Cardone	David Gillett	Lissa LeGrand
Caren E. Carr	Jennifer Gleach	Bill Leonard
Theresa Carver	Jean Gonzalez	Ron Lewis
Noel Catherwold	Louis Graveline	David Locey
David W. Chapman	Pamela Graves	Dennis A. Lockhart
Carol Chiavetta	Jim Greco	Mark D. Loigman
Mitch Christenson	J. Jeff Guice	Marc L. Longlois

Paul Looney
Paige Love
Chris McConnell
Rickey McConnell
Teri D. McConnell
Patti McCrory
John McCullough
Jeff McKay
Greg McMahan
Russell McRae
Tom Maher
Duncan Maio
Becky Manning
Rich Marlow
Paul Marsland
Pat Martin
Ann Mathews
Richard C. Mayfield
Michael Meyer
Susan Mickey
Lauren Miller
Susan Mock
Bob Moeller
Janet Moody
Catherine Moore
Jeff Moore
Martha J. Mountain
Bill Murphree
Michael Neelon
Laurie C. Nicholson
Patricia Noto
Michael Oliver
Mary Ann O'Neal
Frank Ornowski
Charles Otte
Patricia Paine
April Parke
James Parker
Juliella Parsons
Linda S. Pence
Drew Penick
Kathleen Pick
Margery Pierce
Sharon Pierce
Edward T. Ploy
Karen Plunkett
Patricia Porter
Alan Prendergast
Tammy Preston
David Pulliam
Patsy Carol Rainey
Del Walter Rasberg
Glen Reed
Mike Remus
William Rich

Julie Richardson
Henry Riley, III
Arlene Ritz
Sydney Roberts
Jimmy Robertson
Phyllis Robichaud
Lynn Robinson
Sheffield Rogers
Verdery Roosevelt
Cheryl Rosenberg
Stuart Rosenstein
Ginny Ross
James Rugino
Michael S. Russell
Susan Louise Sachs
Robert St. John
Alexine Saunders
Ellen E. Schafroth
Robert Schalau, Jr.
W. Scott Schilk
Sarah Schneiderman
Harve Schulte
Lois Schulte
Susan Schuster
Dan Sedgwick
Barry Sellers
Mark Shanabrough
Lee Ella Shipman-Strong
Barbara Shuefelt
Allison Sinclair
Jennett Sinclair
Glenn Sizemore
Susan Skeen
Darrell H. Smith
Hank Snider
Judith Tucker Snider
Sidney Ann Snyder
Margaret Solod
Karen Spahn
Cathy Spencer
Lynne Marie Spencer
Michael Stedham
Douglas Stetz
Jack Stevens
Don Stockard
Joel Stoehr
Dan Stratman
Laura Sulborski
Stephanie Carol Sultanov
Shannon Sumpter
Will Sweeney
Bill Taffee
Terry F. Tareton
Diana Tatara
Charles G. Taylor, V

Melissa Taylor
Richard Taylor
Barbara Taylorr
John Thigpen
Blair Thomas
Lynn Thompson
Gwendolyn Toth
Ralph Tropf
Tom Tutino
L. Jane Tweed
Bob Upton
Jerry Vance
Gretchen Van Horne
Carol Vick
Rebecca M. Wakefield
Nana Waldrip
Del Walter
Diane Ward
Mary R. Wayne
Diane Webb
Monica Weinzapfel
Susan Weiss
Greg A. West
Bobby White
Myron White
Linda H. Wigley
Pat Williamson
David W. Wills
Tracy Lee Wilson
Pamela Wofford
Robert F. Wolin
Paul Wolking
Susan Wolverton
Martha Wood
Jean Woodall
Jean Woodard
Jerry Wright
Scott Wright
Drew Wyatt
Linda C. Yerina
Alice Young
Ken Young
Phil Young
Sharon Yowell
Pat Mendenhall Yunker
Sylvester Yunker

Artistic Director Martin L. Platt on stage in the new 750-seat Festival Stage with cast members from A Midsummer Night's Dream, *1985.*

Appendix D

ASF HISTORICAL VOLUNTEER LISTING

ASF GUILD PRESIDENTS: Anniston 1972–1984

Tora Johnson, 1984
Alice Donald, 1982–1984
Jean Willett, 1980–1982
Tora Johnson, 1978–1980

Margaret Griffis, 1977–1978
Juliette Doster, 1975–1977
Inga Davis, 1974–1975
Betty Potts, 1973–1974

"I serve here voluntary."

TROILUS AND CRESSIDA

ASF GUILD: 1972–1984

Ludy Abernathy
Joyce Acker
Susan Acker
Bernice Adams
Janice Alig
Peg Anderson
Augusta Andrews
Ethel Andrews
Madelyn Andrews
Edel Ayers
Josephine E. Ayers
Betsy Babb
Emmajon Bagley
Mrs. William Bagley
Anne Bailey
Wynelle Ballard
Vivian Banister
Ann M. Barker
Lynda Barker
Nancy Barker
Nell Bennett
Mary Sue Bernhard
Jean Bibb
Evelyn Black
Carolyn Blount
Virginia Bobbitt
Betty Bolt
Betsy Boze
Beverly Bragg
Eugenia Brannon
Carole Brenner
Lola Bright
Mrs. Ted Broadnax
Pat Brock
Alys Broom
Katherine Brown
Shirley Bryant
Catherine Builder
Jane Burnham
Chris Burns

Rebecca Burt
Margaret Caffey
Patricia Caffey
Peg Caffey
Ida Belle Callahan
Carole Campbell
Sam Canup
Betty Carr
Nancy Carr
Alleen Cater
Irene Cater
Linda Cater
Martha Cater
Carol Cauthen
Barbara Chalk
Susan Cherry
Barbara Childs
Frankie Christenberry
Pat Clark
Mrs. Michael Cleckler
Jeanne Coleman
Sandra Coleman
Ann Collins
Froydis Collins
Evelyn Connors
Evie Connors
Robin Cooper
Frances Couch
Mary Crabtree
Diane Crimmon
Deanie Culver
Marion Currier
Eileen Curtin
Terrye Dachelet
Mrs. Robert Dark
Inga Davis
Mona Davis
Mrs. S. N. Davis
Ann Dean
Wanda Dean

Evelyn Dethlefs
Viorene Detwiler
Anne Deyo
Barry Deyo
Frances diCosola
Maggie Diemart
Alice Donald
Harriett Donoho
Juliette Doster
Judy Draper
Lelie Draper
Irene Duffner
Elizabeth Edwards
Sara Mell Edwards
Mary Jane Eldred
Eleanor Emerson
Katherine Emerson
Becky England
Nancy Eskew
Joan Etnire
Marhea Evans
Betty Faircloth
Sandra Falkenberry
Shelby Fargason
Evelyn Faris
Pam Fite
Mary Louise Flanagan
Hervey Folsom
Helen Forte
Kathy Foster
Marian Foster
Rose Fox
Debra Frame
Katherine Frame
Beanie Freeman
Joyce French
Martha Froelich
Griffin Doster Fry
Mary Fry
Virginia Fulmer

Farley Galbraith
Mary Ann Gann
Mrs. Al C. Garber
Helen Garker
Grace Gates
Susan Gibbins
Minna Glover
Pat Goodgame
Mildred Goodrich
Viola Goodwin
Lois Goodwyn
Selma Gordon
Sara Grant
Elizabeth Grazier
Mrs. C. L. Grebrieaue
Logene Griffin
Margaret Griffis
Mrs. Merlin Hagedorn
Barbara Hall
Kathryn Hamilton
Sara Hammet
Connie Hancock
Mrs. Darwin Hardison
Mary Harris
Terry Harris
Mary Hearn
Jean Held
Faith Hensleigh
Jimmie Hess
Helen Meigs Hill
Ilouise Hill
Miriam Hipp
Carroll Hobbs
Mary Hobbs
Eleanor Holladay
Rosemary Hollingsworth
Beanie Holloway
Lucy Hovius
Jan Howard
Edith Howell
Audrey Howle
Shirley Howze
Hazel Hudson
Mrs. Wilbur B. Hufham
Libby Humphrey
Cissy Hunter
Rissie Ide
Barbara Ingram
Jane Ingram
Lynne Isom
Anne Jackson
Sherlyn Jackson
Anita Jenkins
Kitty Jenkins
Gyung Ja Jin

Emma John
Bette Johns
Anne Johnson
Tora Johnson
Valera Johnson
Katherine Jones
Kay Jones
Margaret Jones
Nan Jones
Rita Judge
Dawn Kell
Janine Kelley
Lalee Kelly
Gail Kemp
Greta Kemp
Madalyn Kemp
Olga Kennedy
Pat Kettles
Betty Ann Key
Popie Kilby
Diane Kimberly
Gena King
Joan King
Martha King
Patty King
Sally King
Tommy King
Anne Kitchin
Anne Klinefelter
Joanne Klinefelter
Mary Lynn Klinefelter
Glenda Knight
Lucy Knight
Bettye Kreh
Jessie Kryder
Carol Kuroski
Betty Lagarde
Marge Lalonde
Helen Laney
Lucy Langworthy
Carlton Lentz
Kirkland Leonard
Maudie Leonard
Craig Lester
Lynn Letson
Harriet Lewis
Mrs. Roger Lienke
Louise Lokey
Gertrude Luther
Judy Mabry
Marion McCallister
Mrs. Terrell McCallister
Deanna McConnell
Diane McCrimmon
Mrs. William McGehee

Jill Mackenzie
Evelyn McMillan
Betty McWhorter
Gale Main
Genevieve Mallory
Sylvia Malone
Judy Manning
Toni Matthews
Becky Merrill
Marguerite Miller
Dorothy Milroy
Anna Minnigerode
Laura Ann Minshew
Virginia Monroe
Ada Montgomery
Gloria Moody
Betty Moore
Ann Morgan
Barbara Morgan
Tee Morgan
Joyce Morrow
Susan Moxley
Charlotte Mullis
Monica Murphy
Julia Murray
Mrs. E. Daniel Nelson
Charlotte Newell
Ridgely Newell
Mrs. Charles Newton, III
Harold Nicrosi
Francys O'Connell
Margot O'Connell
Mrs. Thomas Oliver
Virginia Ordway
Mrs. Charles F. Oudin
Jean Oudin
Alys Owsley
Cathy Pace
Bea Parris
Beverly Parsons
Mrs. J. D. Patrick
Mrs. Rhodes Perdue
Annette Perkins
June Peterson
Mrs. Jack Phillips
Kitty Pickerd
Catherine Pitard
Cathy Pitts
Mrs. Charles Pitts
Judy Poole
Diane Pope
Joanne Pope
Pat Potter
Betty Potts
Jo Propst

"A good heart's worth gold."

HENRY IV, PART TWO

Mabel Quimby
Lillie Rapp
Sharon Rauch
Mrs. Gary Ray
Claudia Reich
Helen Reynolds
Rosalie Reynolds
Lynn Rice
Miggy Rilling
Marguerite Ritchie
Mrs. Cleveland Roberson
Anne Roberts
Diane Roberts
Tyler Roberts
Emily Robison
Maxine Rose
Katherine Rowe
Nancy Lee Rutledge
Bette Saks
Elise Sanguinetti
Lela Sarrell
Mrs. George Scott
Ruth Scruggs
Elizabeth Sellers
Mrs. Joseph Sewell
Adelia Seyforth
Mrs. Robert Shafer
Betty Shannon
Mrs. Carlton Shephard
Lois Sherrill
Christy Skinner
Betty Slate
Sarah Sloan
Carolyn Sloss
Christa Smith
Daisy Weller Smith

Linda G. Smith
Patricia Smith
Rose Smith
Virginia Smith
Oleta Spearman
Jody Speer
Margaret Spidle
Anne Sprayberry
Nettie Springer
Rita Springer
Barbara Sproull
Cyndie Sproull
Brenda Stedham
Mrs. Charles Stephens
Mrs. J. G. Stephens
Carolyn Stewart
Elaine Stewart
Joan Stewart
Judy Stinson
Monica Stoher
Ann Strand
Mrs. H. H. Sumrall
Lynn Talbot
Doris Taylor
Legare Thackston
Mrs. Thomas W. Thagard, Jr.
Emily Thames
Ruth Anne Thompson
Virginia Thompson
Virginia Thrasher
Carol Tipps
Judy Toole
Katherine Tranum
Robin Tucker
Mrs. Robert Turnage
Mable Turner

Marguerite Turner
Beppy Tyler
Abby Ulrey
Jenny Vaughn
Becky Von Settlemyre
Sherrill Waddle
Lily Wallace
Mrs. B. R. Walley
Marge Warren
Muriel Washburn
Willie Welch
Marguerite Wellborn
Betsy West
Sherly West
Jane Wheeler
Elise White
Sarah Whitson
Mim Wickstrom
Jean Willett
Bett Williams
Irene Williams
Nan Williams
Angela Williamson
Bobbie Wilson
Mrs. Clyde Wilson
Marge Wilson
Patricia Wingo
Enid Winson
Kathleen Wood
Jean Woodall
Flora Woodruff
Harriet Woodruff
Penny Young

A side view of the new ASF Complex in Montgomery.

WILL'S GUILD

ASF Volunteers in Montgomery   September 1985

President   Kathy Conely
President-Elect   Joyce Faye Cox
First Vice-President   Winnie Goodwyn
Second Vice-President   Nancy Seale
Recording Secretary   Caroll Missildine
Corresponding Secretary   Terry Kohn
Treasurer   Cathy Byrd

From left to right are Nancy Seale, Winnie Goodwyn, Katherine Conely, and Cathy Byrd from Montgomery's 1985 Will's Guild.

WILL'S GUILD MEMBERS

Karen Adkison	Mrs. W. A. Daniel	Tricia Jackson
Martha Alexander	Monda Davis	Donna Johnson
Richard Anderson	Sandra W. Davis	Lucille Jones
Roy Anderson	Lander Dean	Shay Jones
Jackie Aronov	Hendan DeBray	Margaret Jordan
Alexia Bailey	Margaret Delahay	Liza Kaufman
Carol Ballard	A. Wayne DeLoach	Sam Kaufman
Jean Baranowski	Donna DePhilippis	Ouita Kimbrough
Mary Jo Barnes	Teri Diamond	Sally Kimbrough
Betty Beale	Frances Durr	Terry Kohn
Jayonn Bearden	Susan Edwards	Joy Lambert
Charlotte Beck	Jean Elebash	Mary Lancaster
Lynn Beshear	Elizabeth Emmet	Barbara Larson
Joy Blondheim	Gail Eulenstein	Carolyn LeFleur
Jane Blount	Betty Fenton	Betty Loeb
Lucy Blount	Marcie Flinn	Joan Loeb
Faye Blue	Jane Forshey (Allen)	Nancy Loeb
Jonathon Bowman	Betsy Forster	Jeannie Duke Loop
Bob Braco	Betty Foshee	Jim Loop
Nancy Bradford	Marjorie Fulton	Mollie Luskin
Elizabeth Brantley	Maxine Goldner	Debbie McInnis
Nancy W. Brooks	Winnie Goodwyn	Cheryl McKiearnan
Mary Brown	Hester Gordon	Peggy Mann
Maureen Brown	John Gorrie	Ed Martin
Carol Butler	Jo Ann Gosnell	Mary Ann Martin
Marion Butler	Betty Goyer	Jean Mattox
Cathy Byrd	Anne Graham	Carroll Missildine
Martha Cameron	Emily Graham	Winnie Mitchell
Betty Campbell	John Guerrieri	Candy Morris
Boyd Campbell	Dottie Hanan	Sue Norgard
Louise Candler	Patsy Hatcher	Emma Norris
Clare Cardinal	Frederick W. Herbst	Dr. Harry Ohme
Brenda Carr	Janice H. Hersman	Susie Oliver
Edie Chappell	Ilouise Hill	Sandra Parnell
Dee Coleman	Jean Hinds	Carol Patton
Katherine Conely	Truman Hobbs, Jr.	Jule Perry
Lesley Cooper	Jan Howard	Lou Perryman
Joyce Faye Cox	Sue Howard	Kay Pilgreen
Rodney V. Cox	Mrs. Hamilton Hutchinson	Beth Powell
Rosalie Cox	Brenda Ives	Martha Rankin

Eve Shearer at the first major Will's Guild meeting at the Capri Theatre in Montgomery, Alabama (1985).

ASF staff and university leaders work to plan "Theatre in the Mind" programs with staff from the Alabama Humanities Foundation.

Mari J. Reed-Berry
Betty Robinson
Sarah Roche
Heflin Sanders
Judy Sanders
Florence Savler
Esther Scheuer
Nancy Seale
Bessie Shackelford
Eve Shearer
Kitty Sheehan
Lisa Shivers
Jane Sims

Baldwin Smith
Barbara H. Smith
Judy Stark
Ken Stephens
Mary Stephens
Sylvia Strickland
Susan Strong
Margaret Sturgis
Dianne Teague
Patti Thompson
Diane Thomson
Heather L. Toellner
Mary Dixon Torbery

Anna Marie Troy
Patricia Tuttle
Grace Warner
Jinnie Webster
Dyann Wilkerson
M. P. Wilkerson
Diane Williams
Jane Wimberley
Eloise P. Winfield
Glenn A. Yates
Joy J. Yates
Charlotte Yonclas
Betty Jane Young

Artistic Director Martin L. Platt, Managing Director Jim Volz, and educators Jim White and Bill Matthews.

Appendix E

FINANCIAL SUMMARIES

GENERAL FINANCIAL HISTORY
Alabama Shakespeare Festival, The State Theatre

YEAR	TOTAL EXPENSE	TOTAL INCOME	SURPLUS (DEFICIT)
1972	$ 8,000	$ 7,966	(34)
1973	23,890	21,100	(2,790)
1974	32,140	42,005	9,865
1975	50,466	48,862	(1,604)
1976	77,550	85,239	7,689
1977	125,444	114,721	(10,723)
1978	252,374	253,227	853
1979	410,694	409,197	1,497
1980	542,449	505,873	(36,576)
1981	785,887	736,098	(49,789)
1982	694,769	677,161	(17,608)
1983	759,685	1,024,604	264,919
1984*	792,677	836,867	44,190

*9 months

EARNED INCOME HISTORY
Alabama Shakespeare Festival, The State Theatre

YEAR	SUMMER BOX OFFICE	SUBSIDIARY EARNED INCOME	TOUR BOOKINGS	TOTAL EARNED INCOME
1972	4,250	216	N/A	4,466
1973	10,337	756	N/A	11,093
1974	20,528	11,617	N/A	32,145
1975	27,405	9,194	N/A	36,599
1976	30,624	20,976	N/A	51,600
1977	53,543	19,403	N/A	72,946
1978	90,558	31,343	65,000	186,901
1979	121,645	43,603	106,455	271,703
1980	166,612	52,246	142,794	361,652
1981	185,148	63,142	128,017	376,307
1982	201,506	40,480	189,725	431,711
1983	247,600	65,313	200,900	513,813
1984*	208,674	54,867	58,085	321,626

*9 months

"They say if money go before, all ways do lie open."

THE MERRY WIVES OF WINDSOR

Peg Brady "paints" a costume in the new ASF complex in Montgomery.

UNEARNED INCOME HISTORY
Alabama Shakespeare Festival, The State Theatre

YEAR	CONTRIBUTIONS	GRANTS	OTHER	TOTAL UNEARNED INCOME
1972	1,000	2,500		3,500
1973	6,507	3,500		10,007
1974	7,060	2,800		9,860
1975	10,513	1,750		12,263
1976	10,389	23,250		33,639
1977	21,682	18,000		39,682
1978	28,927	37,399		66,326
1979	55,531	81,963		137,494
1980	70,361	73,860		144,221
1981	87,080	10,000	262,711	359,791
1982	203,976	41,479		245,450
1983	308,370	146,625	55,796	510,791
1984*	241,857	67,300	206,084	515,241

*9 months

TOTAL INCOME HISTORY
Alabama Shakespeare Festival, The State Theatre

YEAR	TOTAL INCOME	PERCENTAGE INCREASE OVER PREVIOUS YEAR
1972	7,966	N/A
1973	21,100	164.88%
1974	42,005	99.08%
1975	48,862	16.32%
1976	85,239	74.45%
1977	114,721	34.59%
1978	253,227	120.73%
1979	409,197	38.12%
1980	505,873	23.63%
1981	736,098	45.51%
1982	677,161	(8.7%)
1983	1,024,604	51.31%
1984*	836,867	(18.32%)

*9 months

"I can raise no money by vile means."

JULIUS CAESAR

EXPENSE HISTORY
Alabama Shakespeare Festival, The State Theatre

YEAR	ARTISTIC SALARIES	NON-ARTISTIC SALARIES	PRODUCTION EXPENSES	ADMINISTRATIVE EXPENSES	TOTAL EXPENSES
1972	1,000	0	5,500	1,500	8,000
1973	5,320	700	8,162	9,708	23,890
1974	6,300	800	5,950	19,090	32,140
1975	18,409	4,000	9,566	18,491	50,466
1976	30,569	8,850	14,087	24,044	77,550
1977	46,217	20,816	22,541	35,870	125,444
1978	94,308	35,606	30,304	92,156	252,374
1979	186,559	48,821	32,488	142,824	410,694
1980	213,983	76,975	43,623	207,868	542,449
1981	277,610	127,000	70,947	310,330	785,887
1982	163,351	148,517	116,439	266,462	694,769
1983	243,969	161,829	133,000	220,887	759,685
1984*	112,043	85,863	447,013	147,758	792,677

*9 months

Appendix F

A CHRONOLOGY OF SHAKESPEARE'S PLAYS

YEAR	PLAY	ASF PRODUCTION DATE
1588–93	*The Comedy of Errors*	1972–1978–1983 (Tour)
1588–94	*Love's Labour's Lost*	1977–1984
1590–91	*Henry VI, Part 2*	
1590–91	*Henry VI, Part 3*	
1591–92	*Henry VI, Part 1*	
1592–93	*Richard III*	1986
1592–94	*Titus Andronicus*	
1593–94	*The Taming of the Shrew*	1974–1978–1983
1593–95	*Two Gentlemen of Verona*	1972–1980 (Tour)
1594–96	*Romeo and Juliet*	1974–1980–1982 (Tour)
1595	*Richard II*	1975
1594–96	*A Midsummer Night's Dream*	1974–1981–1985
1596–97	*King John*	
1596–97	*The Merchant of Venice*	1978
1597	*Henry IV, Part 1*	1981
1597–98	*Henry IV, Part 2*	
1598–99	*Henry V*	
1598–1600	*Much Ado About Nothing*	1973–1981
1599	*Julius Caesar*	
1599–1600	*As You Like It*	1973–1979
1599–1600	*Twelfth Night*	1975–1979–1982
1600–01	*Hamlet*	1972–1977–1982
1597–1601	*Merry Wives of Windsor*	1976–1986
1601–02	*Troilus and Cressida*	
1602–04	*All's Well That Ends Well*	1983
1603–04	*Othello*	1978
1604	*Measure for Measure*	1978
1605–06	*King Lear*	1976–1983
1605–06	*Macbeth*	1973–1979–1984
1606–07	*Antony and Cleopatra*	
1605–08	*Timon of Athens*	
1607–09	*Coriolanus*	
1608–09	*Pericles*	
1609–10	*Cymbeline*	1980
1610–11	*The Winter's Tale*	1976
1611	*The Tempest*	1975
1612–13	*Henry VIII*	

"Can one desire too much of a good thing?"

AS YOU LIKE IT

Nancy Knott works in the ASF scene shop, carving a statue used onstage for the 1985–86 production of A Midsummer Night's Dream.

Appendix G

MEMBERS OF THE ASF CONSORTIUM FOR ACADEMIC PROGRAMS

"O Lord, I could have stay'd here all the night to hear good counsel: O, what learning is!"

ROMEO AND JULIET

OFFICERS

Dr. Guin A. Nance, PRESIDENT
Vice Chancellor for Academic Affairs
Auburn University at Montgomery

Dr. Edward C. Moore, SECRETARY
Senior Vice Chancellor
The University of Alabama System

Dr. Edmond Williams, CHAIRMAN OF THE GRADUATE COMMITTEE
Chairman, Department of Theatre and Dance
The University of Alabama

Dr. Charles C. Harbour, CHAIRMAN OF THE UNDERGRADUATE COMMITTEE
Chairman, Department of Communication Arts
University of Montevallo

INSTITUTIONAL REPRESENTATIVES

Alabama A & M University
  James Vinson
Alabama State University
  Bertram Martin
  Michael Howley
Athens State College
  Penne Laubenthal
  Elva McLin
Auburn University
  Lois Garren
  Jon Walker
Auburn University at Montgomery
  James R. Williams
  Guin A. Nance
  Wiley Boyles
  Marion C. Michael
  Bob Gaines
Birmingham-Southern College
  Susan Hagen
Huntingdon College
  Robert Barmettler
Judson College
  Wanda Raley
  Charley Ann Reichley
Livingston University
  Roy Underwood
  James McGahey
Samford University
  Margaret O. Brodnax
  Harold Hunt

Troy State University
  O. David Dye
Tuskegee Institute
  Thomas M. Curran
The University of Alabama
  Douglas Jones
  E. Roger Sayers
  Edmond Williams
The University of Alabama at Birmingham
  Theodore Benditt
  Ward Haarbauer
  Robert Yowell
University of Alabama System
  Edward C. Moore
The University of Alabama in Huntsville
  John Mebane
  Robert Welker
  Paul Webb
The University of Montevallo
  Charles C. Harbour
University of North Alabama
  Joseph Thomas
  William Foster
  John Roth
University of South Alabama
  R. Eugene Jackson
Alabama Shakespeare Festival
  Martin L. Platt
  Jim Volz

Appendix H

CITY, COUNTY, AND STATE GOVERNMENT LEADERS

COUNCIL OF THE CITY OF MONTGOMERY, Mayor Emory Folmar

E. T. Chambers, *President pro tem*
Herchel M. Christian
Joseph Dickerson
Mark Gilmore, Jr.
Leu W. Hammonds
William P. Nunn, III
Joe L. Reed
Mrs. Alice D. Reynolds, *President*
Billy M. Turner

MONTGOMERY COUNTY COMMISSIONERS

Joel W. Barfoot, *Chairman*
Frank A. Bray
W. F. Joseph
John F. Knight
Mack O. McWhorter

ALABAMA LEGISLATURE

Governor George C. Wallace
Lieutenant Governor Bill Baxley
Secretary of the Senate McDowell Lee

SENATORS

Gary L. Aldridge	Ryan deGraffenried, Jr.	William Fred Horn
John E. Amari	Bobby Denton	Charles D. Langford
Chip Bailey	Gerald O. Dial	Ted Little
Lowell Barron	Larry Dixon	William J. Menton
Roger Bedford, Jr.	Bill Drinkard	Hinton Mitchem
Ann Bedsole	Frank Ellis, Jr.	Mac Parsons
Jim Bennett	Michael A. Figures	Hank Sanders
Charles Dean Bishop	E. Crum Foshee	Bill G. Smith
W. J. Cabaniss, Jr.	Earl Goodwin	Jim Smith
Steve Cooley	Perry A. Hand	Frances Strong
Danny Corbett	Earl F. Hilliard	John A. Teague
J. Foy Covington, Jr.	Donald G. Holmes	

REPRESENTATIVES

Charles Adams	Spencer Bachus	Greg Beers
Robert E. Albright	John P. Beasley	Jack Biddle, III

Governor George C. Wallace, a major supporter of the arts in Alabama, arrives to assist in the ASF dedication.

Lucius Black
A. J. Blake
Harrell Blakeney
Hugh Boles
W. C. Bowling
Michael E. Box
Carl C. Brakefield
Charlie Britnell
Morris J. Brooks, Jr.
Glen Browder
Jenkins Bryant, Jr.
June Bugg
Ralph Burke
James E. Buskey
John L. Buskey
Tom Butler
James M. Campbell
Joe R. Carothers, Jr.
Tommy Carter
Denzel L. Clark
James S. (Jimmy) Clark
William Clark
Tom C. Coburn
T. Loyd Coleman
W. F. Cosby, Jr.
Bobby C. Crow
Patricia Davis
Roger D. Dutton
Sundra E. Escott
Dwight Faulk
Steve Flowers
Joe Ford
William P. Fuller, Jr.

Victor Gaston
J. W. Goodwin
Billy Gray
George W. Grayson
E. A. Grouby, Jr.
Albert Hall
Seth Hammett
Taylor F. Harper
Bob Harvey
Steve Hettinger
Jimmy W. Holley
Alvin Holmes
Perry O. Hooper, Jr.
Ronald G. Johnson, Jr.
Roy W. Johnson, Jr.
Bobby M. Junkins
Yvonne Kennedy
Ken Kvalheim
Richard J. Laird
Jack B. Lauderdale
Richard J. Lindsey
Bobbie G. McDowell
Bob McKee
Stephen A. McMillan
Chris McNair
Beth Marietta
Charles B. Martin
Nathan Mathis
Bryant Melton
Mike Mikell
Earl Mitchell
Otis H. Moore
Max Newman

Tom Nicholson
Mike Onderdonk
Paul Parker
Arthur Payne
Walter E. Penry, Jr.
George Perdue
Phil Poole
Jack E. Pratt
James E. Preuitt
T. Euclid Rains
Thomas Reed
John W. Rice
Ben T. Richardson
John W. Rogers, Jr.
James G. Sasser
George G. Seibels, Jr.
Curtis Smith
Lewis G. Spratt
Nelson R. Starkey, Jr.
John C. Starr, Jr.
John F. Tanner
James L. Thomas
Hoyt W. Trammell
J. E. Turner
Pete Turnham
Jack B. Venable
James E. Warren
Frank P. White
Gary White
Thomas Lester White
Mary S. Zoghby

"Love talks with better knowledge,
and knowledge with dearer love."

MEASURE FOR MEASURE

Appendix I

ASF PHOTOGRAPHER CREDITS

Photographs for this publication are taken from Alabama Shakespeare Festival files. Photographers from 1972 through 1986 include:

James Adams
The Anniston Chamber of Commerce
The Anniston Star
Dan Carraco
William Davis
Michael Doege
Ken Elkins
Stephen Gross
Jerry Harris
Timothy Hursley
Danny Hurt
Jim Johnson

Glenda Knight
Patricia Lavender
Spider Martin
Carmel Modica
Michelle R. Moore
Michael Overton
Martin L. Platt
Charles M. Rafshoon
Robert C. Ragsdale, F.R.P.S.
Robertson Photography
Louis Sohn
Jim Volz

A Tribute to
Winton M. "Red" and Carolyn Blount

The generous gift of the new ASF complex to the State of Alabama saved the State Theatre from almost certain extinction and marks one of the most significant arts contributions in the history of American giving to a single regional theatre.

Members of the Blount family could inspire book after book. However, the best insight into the origin of this beautiful theatre may be found in Winton M. Blount's own words:

Business has become more keenly aware of the environment in which it functions—the human context of our businesses. It has played, and must continue to play, a significant role in support of education, public and human affairs, and the arts.

The national drive toward a better life, it seems to me, is slowly shifting back to the community level. The quality of our cities was neglected for several decades, and we are realizing now that was a mistake. We know now that cities don't just grow and get better. They have to be made better—by people, for people.

It may be difficult to define the exact role of the arts in our community life, although we are increasingly aware of their importance. Obviously the arts have much to do with the quality of life. Museums and their activities offer a tangible beauty and cultural spirit that are essential to our city, in both an economic and a human sense. The presence of cultural activities is a potent force in helping to make a city attractive to the new breed of college graduates and younger people who have a strong social and cultural awareness.

So it is a matter of enlightened self-interest for business to support the arts. And it is a matter of good corporate citizenship. But most of all, it is a matter of making our community a better place to live for those of us who take great pride in calling it home.

Winton M. Blount
Chairman of the Board and Chief Executive Officer
Blount, Inc.

"What impossible matters will he make easy next?"

THE TEMPEST

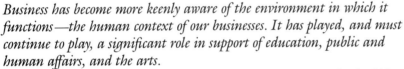

Acknowledgments

A grateful acknowledgment must go to Evelyn Carol Case, Dr. Albert H. Nadeau, Dr. Richard Knaub, Dr. Martin Cobin, Jack Volz, Betty Volz, and the ASF Staff, Guild, and Board of Directors who helped make this work possible.

A special thank you to John Kelly, Juliette Doster, Abe J. Bassett, Inga and Bill Davis, Austin Letson, E. Guice Potter, Tom Stinson, Bill Talbot, Red and Carolyn Blount, Abby and Jim Ulrey, Josephine E. and H. Brandt Ayers, Philip A. and Caroline Sellers, Jean Willett, and Alice Donald, whose personal and professional support and confidence helped make miracles happen in Alabama.

Finally, this book and the happy news that it contains would not have been possible without the assistance of many dedicated staff members, only a few of whom are listed here:

Esther Bloomfield	Patricia Lavender
Nancy Carmichael	Mark Loigman
Benjamin Condray	Carol Ogus
Donni Cooper	Doug Perry
Steven Cornwell	Martin L. Platt
Jim Donadio	Eve Shearer
Jay Drury	Larry Stafford
Lori Grifo	Linda Tucker
Barbara Larson	

"Love's reason without reason."

CYMBELINE

The title: *Shakespeare Never Slept Here,* courtesy of Carol Ogus.

JIM VOLZ is the Managing Director and Chief Executive Officer of the Alabama Shakespeare Festival. A native of Dayton, Ohio, Dr. Volz has a varied background that includes positions as journalist, photographer, counselor, business manager, artistic director, and university professor.

Devoted to theatre education, Dr. Volz has taught at six universities and has visited and studied theatres throughout the United States, Canada, and Western Europe. His formal education includes a B.A. from Wright State University, an M.A. from Bowling Green State University, and a Ph.D. from the University of Colorado, Boulder.

Prior to joining the ASF in 1982, Dr. Volz taught acting and theatre management at the University of Colorado in Boulder and consulted with a number of professional arts groups in Colorado. In 1982, the ASF Board of Directors and Artistic Director Martin L. Platt contracted Volz to spearhead the ASF's transition from a summer operation in Anniston, Alabama, to year-round production in the new Montgomery complex.

"The immediate quality that Jim brought to ASF was steadiness and firmness in management," explains Platt. "Jim quickly took control, imposed strict financial controls, and pulled the ASF, truly singlehandedly, from deep red ink to black ink and a clean slate as one of America's strongest theatre operations."

According to longtime Board member Austin Letson, "Jim Volz's administrative abilities rate with the best that I have ever seen in the arts or other business for that matter. His ability to teach and educate is also a very strong quality. The Alabama Shakespeare Festival would certainly not be the dynamic organization that it is today without the expert guidance of Jim Volz."

Dr. Volz has served as a theatre consultant for many of the nation's theatres, is an active member of nearly a dozen professional organizations, and was recently appointed to the steering committee for the American Council on the Arts.

In the past few years, Volz has devoted his spare time to writing plays, improving racquetball skills, skiing or hiking almost half of the Rocky Mountains, and writing for publication.

Dr. Volz is married to actress Evelyn Carol Case, who precedes him as a member of the ASF company.

Carter, Tommy, 156
Carver, Theresa, *88*, 140, 144
Case, Evelyn Carol, vii, *21, 33, 34, 36, 44, 52, 70, 71, 74, 110, 122,* 139, 140, 158
Case, Lou, *113*
Caserta, Ida, 140
Casey, Beulah, 140, 142
Casteel, Karen, 140
Cater, Alleen, 146
Cater, Irene, 146
Cater, Linda, 146
Cater, Martha, 146
Catherwold, Noel, 144
Cauthen, Carol, 146
Chalk, Barbara, 146
Chambers, E. T., 106, 155
Chandler, Kathy, 140, 142
Chapman, David W., 144
Chappell, Edie, 149
Chappell, Fred, 135, 139
Chase, Marydith, 139
Cheatham, Stacey, 142
Chenette, Mary Ellen, 142
Cherry, Susan, 146
Chiavetta, Carol, 144
Childs, Barbara, 146
Childs, John, 98, 100, 102
Christenberry, Frankie, 146
Christenson, Mitch, 144
Christian, Herchel M., 106, 155
chronology, historical, 127–131
chronology of plays, audience statistics, and budgets, 132–138
chronology of Shakespeare's plays, 153
Clarence Darrow (Rintels), 30, 128, 135
Clark, Denzel L., 156
Clark, James S., 156
Clark, Judy, 142
Clark, Pat, 146
Clark, Scott, 142
Clark, William, 156
Clarke, Mary Katherine, 142
Clavelli, Christopher, 140
Cleckler, Michael H., 144
Cleckler, Mrs. Michael, 146
Cleveland, Fran, 100, 102
Coates, Thom, 144
Coats, Stacy, 118, 142
Cobb, Steve, 144
Cobin, Martin, 158
Coburn, Tom C., 156
Coca-Cola Company, 117
Cochran, Pat, 144
Cockrell, Quinton, 140
Coe, Richard L., 62, 129
Coker, Robert, 142
Cole, Andrew, 140
Cole, Rob, 140
Coleman, Dee, 149
Coleman, Jeanne, 146
Coleman, Lori Lee, 144

Coleman, Sandra, 146
Coleman, T. Loyd, 156
Collier, Bruce, 140
Collins, Ann, 146
Collins, Froydis, 146
Collins, Joe, 139
Comedy of Errors, The, 3, 6, 7, 40, 58, 66, *71,* 127, 132, 135, 136, 137, 153
Comer, Jane S., *101, 102*
Committee for the Humanities, 62, 110, 130
Condray, Becky, 142
Condray, Benjamin, 142, 158
Cone, Tom, 139
Conely, Anne, 142
Conely, David, 142
Conely, Jim, 139
Conely, Katherine, 149
Conery, Edward, 140
Connors, Evelyn, 146
Connors, Evie, 146
Consortium for Academic Programs, 108–109, 130, 131, 154
Cook, Bruce, 19
Cook, Christine A., 144
Cook, Ron, 144
Cooley, Steve, 155
Coonrod, Frances, *113*
Cooper, Donni, 118, 142, 158
Cooper, Lesley, 149
Cooper, Robin, 146
Corbett, Danny, 155
Corbley, Kate, 144
Coriolanus, 153
Cornwell, Steve, 142, 158
Cosby, W. F., Jr., 156
Cotner, Stefan, *12,* 140
Cotten, James, 140
Couch, Frances, 146
Country Wife, The (Wycherley), 135
Coutts, Deborah, 144
Cover, A. D., *21, 73, 74, 76, 77, 80, 88,* 140
Covington, J. Foy, Jr., 155
Cowan, John A., 144
Cowperthwaite, Joseph, 142
Cox, Elizabeth, 142
Cox, Joyce Faye, 149
Cox, Robert, 140
Cox, Rodney V., 149
Cox, Rosalie, 149
Cox, Susan A., 139
Cox, Walter, 110
Crabtree, Mary, 146
Craft, Robert H., Jr., *101, 102*
Crane, Lorraine, 144
Crean, Jean, 140
Crew, Kyle, 144
Crimmon, Diane, 146
Crofton, Louise, 139
Cromer, Bruce, *16, 33, 37, 38, 56, 64, 65, 66, 80, 95, 110, 122,* 139, 140

Crotty, Patricia, 142
Crow, Bobby C., 156
Crow, Kim, 140
Crysel, Amy, 142
Crysel, Barbara, 142
Culbreth, Ron, 140
Culver, Deanie, 146
Cunningham, Emory, 100, 102
Curran, Thomas M., 154
Currier, Marion, 146
Curtin, Eileen, 146
Cymbeline, 33, 48, 135, 153

Dachelet, Terrye, 146
Daniel, Mrs. W. A., 149
Dark, Mrs. Robert, 146
Daughtry, Rob, 144
David, Charslyn, 142
Davis, Inga, *2,* 98, 100, 102, *103,* 146, 158
Davis, Mona, 146
Davis, Monda, 149
Davis, Patricia, 156
Davis, Mrs. S. N., 146
Davis, Sandra W., 149
Davis, William J., 23, *90,* 91, 92, 98, 100, 102, 127, 142, 156, 158
Dawson, Taylor, 100, 102
Dean, Ann, 146
Dean, Lander, 149
Dean, Wanda, 146
Death of a Salesman (Miller), 119, 138
DeBevc, Joe, 140
DeBray, Hendan, 149
Degas, Andre, 140
de Havilland, Olivia, *107, 112, 133*
deGraffenried, Ryan, Jr., 155
Delahay, Margaret, 149
Dell, Kathryn, 140, 142, 144
DeLoach, A. Wayne, 149
Dent, Hilda, 144
Denton, Bobby, 155
DePhilippis, Donna, 149
Depoy, Scott, 140
DeRagon, Pierre, 144
Dethlefs, Evelyn, 146
Detwiler, Viorene, 146
DeVille, Douglas, 144
DeVille, Eileen, 144
deWitt-Howard, Sherrill, 144
Deyo, Anne, 146
Deyo, Barry, 146
Deyo, George, 102
Dial, Gerald O., 155
Diamond, Teri, 149
Dickerson, Joseph, 106, 155
diCosola, Frances, 146
Diemart, Maggie, 146
Dixon, Larry, 155
Dobson, Will, 144
Doege, Marsha Coleman, 142
Doege, Michael, 142, 156

Design and Production
Faith Nance
Design for Publishing/Birmingham, Alabama

Editor
Lynn Carter
Birmingham, Alabama

Indexer
Alexa Selph
Atlanta, Georgia

Composition
Typeface/Galliard
Graphic Composition/Athens, Georgia

Color Separations
Classic Color/Atlanta, Georgia

Printing and Binding
R.R. Donnelly and Sons, Co./Chicago, Illinois

Paper
Sterling Web Dull
Westvaco/Atlanta, Georgia

Endleaves
Rainbow
Narragansett Coated Papers/Pawtucket, Rhode Island

Cover Cloth
Kingston Natural Finish
Holliston Mills/Hyannis, Massachusetts